D1154974

HORROR OF THE HEIGHTS

BY ANTHONY MASTERS

ILLUSTRATED BY PETER DENNIS
COVER ILLUSTRATION BY BRETT HAWKINS
COLORS BY BRETT HAWKINS

LIBRARIAN REVIEWER
Chris Kreie
Media Specialist, Eden Prairie Schools, MN
MS in Information Media, St. Cloud State University, MN

READING CONSULTANT
Mary Evenson
Middle School Teacher, Edina Public Schools, MN
MA in Education, University of Minnesota, MN

STONE ARCH BOOKS
Minneapolis San Diego

First published in the United States in 2006
by Stone Arch Books,
151 Good Counsel Drive, P.O. Box 669,
Mankato, Minnesota 56002.

Originally published in Great Britain in 2001
by A & C Black Publishers Ltd.

Library of Congress Cataloging-in-Publication Data
Masters, Anthony.
    Horror of the Heights / by Anthony Masters; illustrated by Peter Dennis.
    p. cm. — (Graphic Quest)
    ISBN-13: 978-1-59889-030-3 (hardcover)
    ISBN-10: 1-59889-030-1 (hardcover)
    1. Graphic novels. I. Dennis, Peter, 1950- II. Title. III. Series.
PN6727.M246H67 2006
741.5—dc22   2005026596

Summary: Dean Lambert suffers from a fear of heights — a big deal if your brother
is a diving champion and your father runs the Wave Crest Health Club. Someone is
out to sabotage the diving board that Dean fears. He needs to expose the saboteur for
everyone's sake.

1 2 3 4 5 6 11 10 09 08 07 06

Printed in the United States of America.

TABLE OF CONTENTS

CHAPTER ONE

Dean Lambert gazed up at the "Horror of the Heights." That's what he had nicknamed the high-diving board at the Wave Crest Health Club. Now he was determined to conquer his fear.

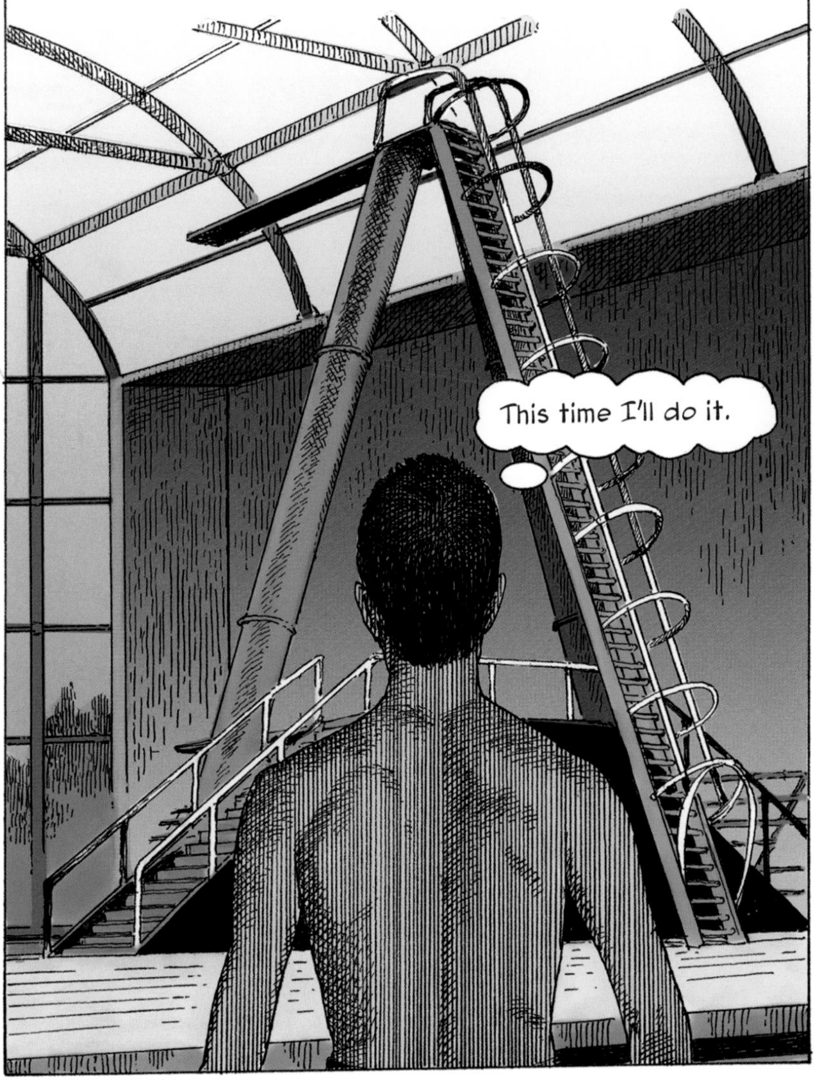
This time I'll do it.

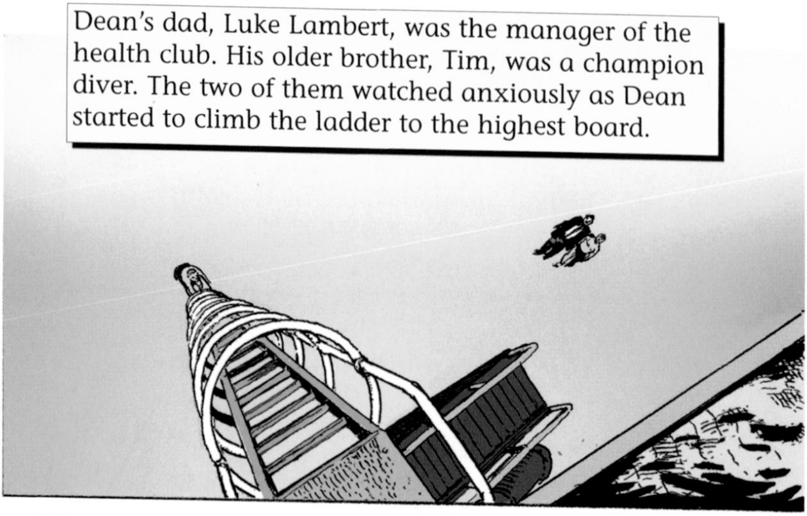
Dean's dad, Luke Lambert, was the manager of the health club. His older brother, Tim, was a champion diver. The two of them watched anxiously as Dean started to climb the ladder to the highest board.

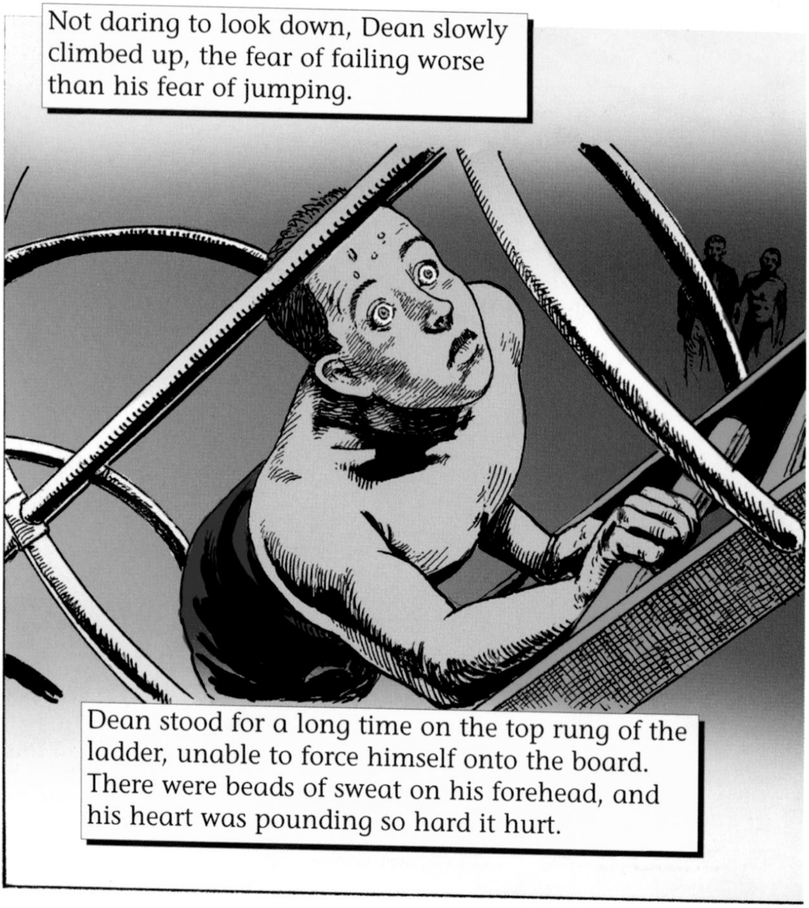
Not daring to look down, Dean slowly climbed up, the fear of failing worse than his fear of jumping.
Dean stood for a long time on the top rung of the ladder, unable to force himself onto the board. There were beads of sweat on his forehead, and his heart was pounding so hard it hurt.

He glanced down, only to see his dad and Tim staring up at him, urging him on. They both wanted him to succeed.

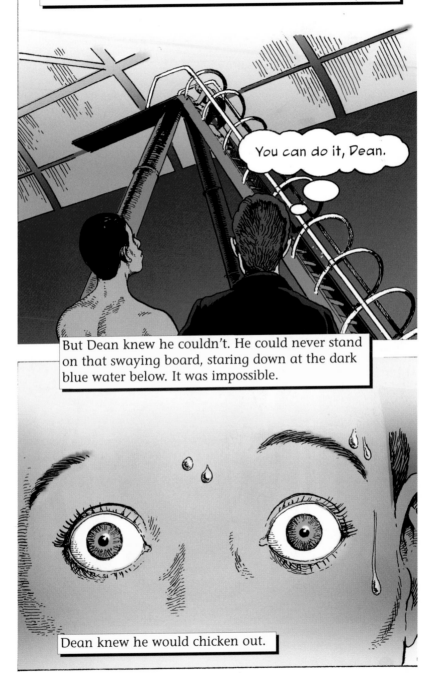

You can do it, Dean.

But Dean knew he couldn't. He could never stand on that swaying board, staring down at the dark blue water below. It was impossible.

Dean knew he would chicken out.

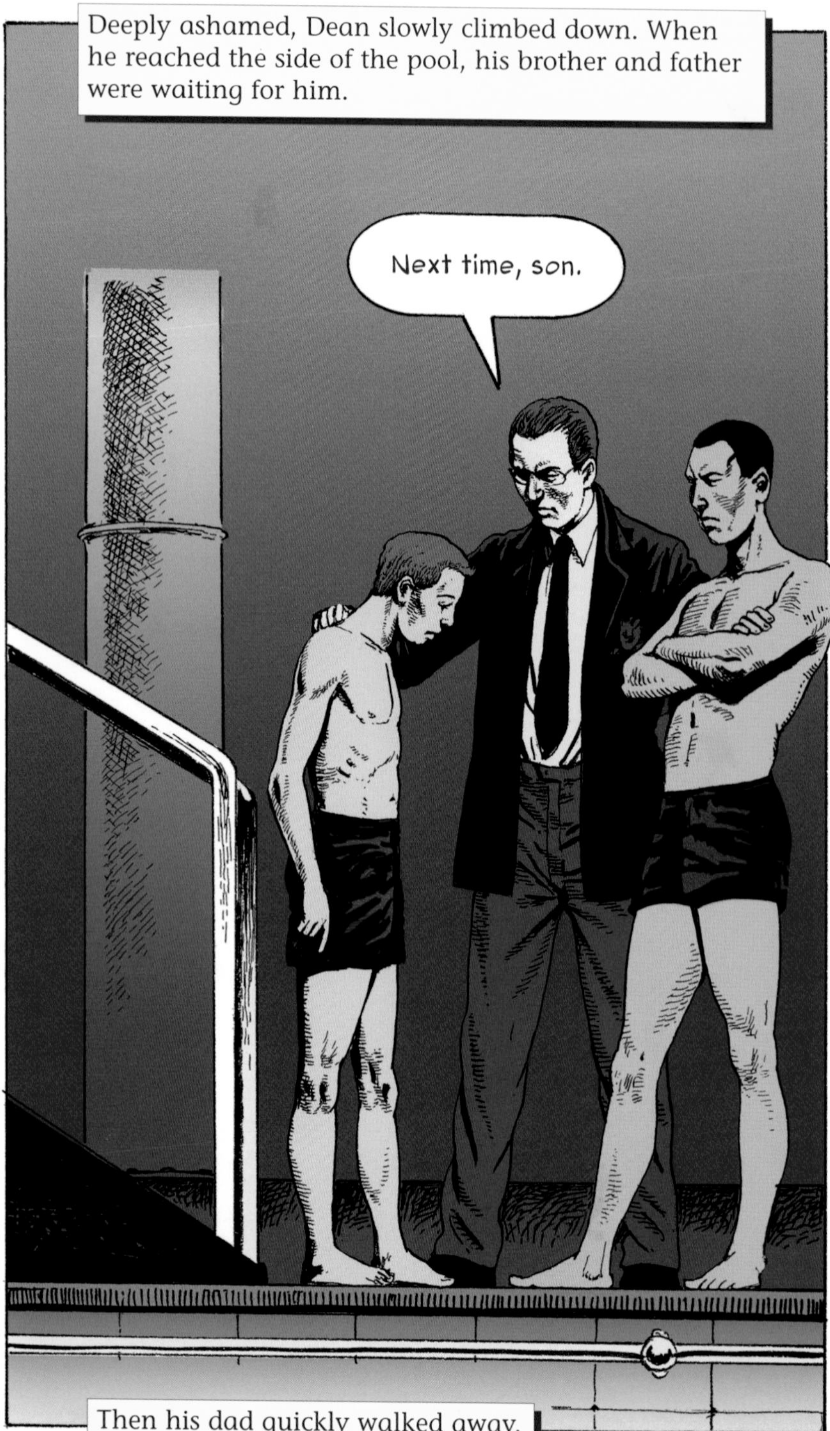
Deeply ashamed, Dean slowly climbed down. When he reached the side of the pool, his brother and father were waiting for him.
Next time, son.
Then his dad quickly walked away.

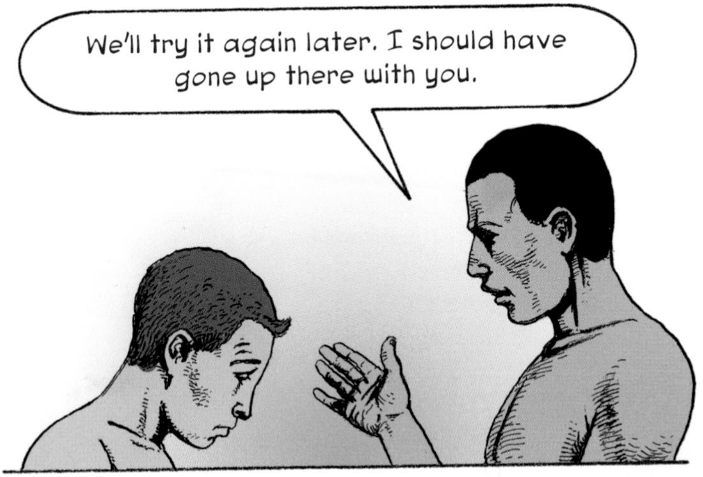
We'll try it again later. I should have gone up there with you.

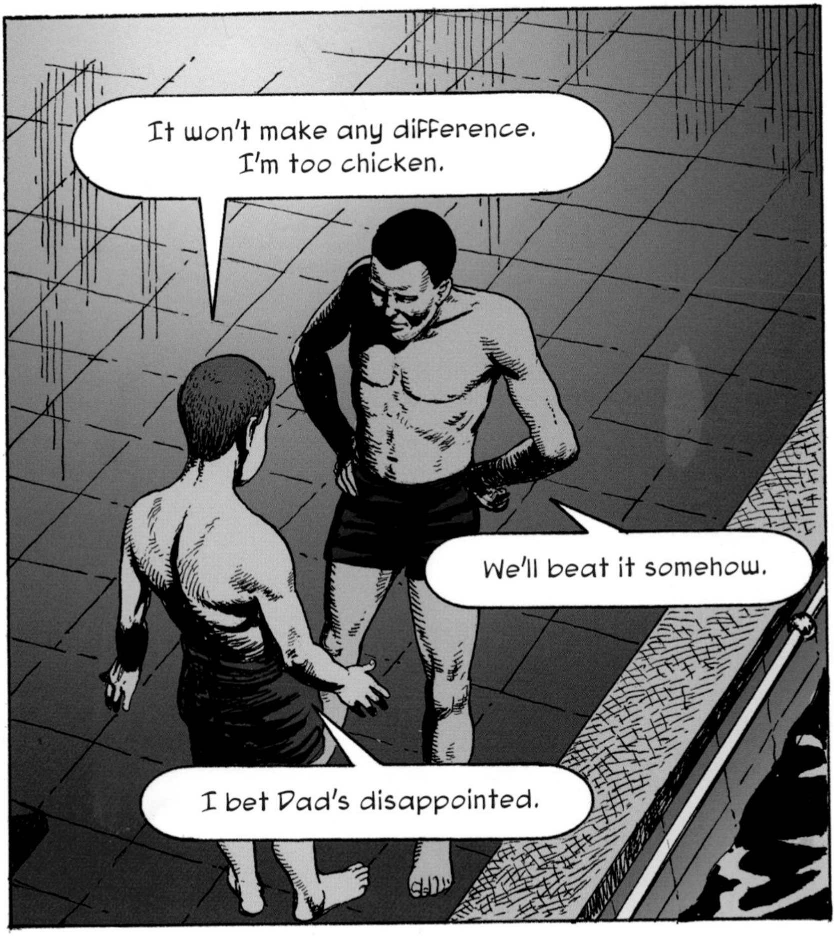
It won't make any difference. I'm too chicken.
We'll beat it somehow.
I bet Dad's disappointed.

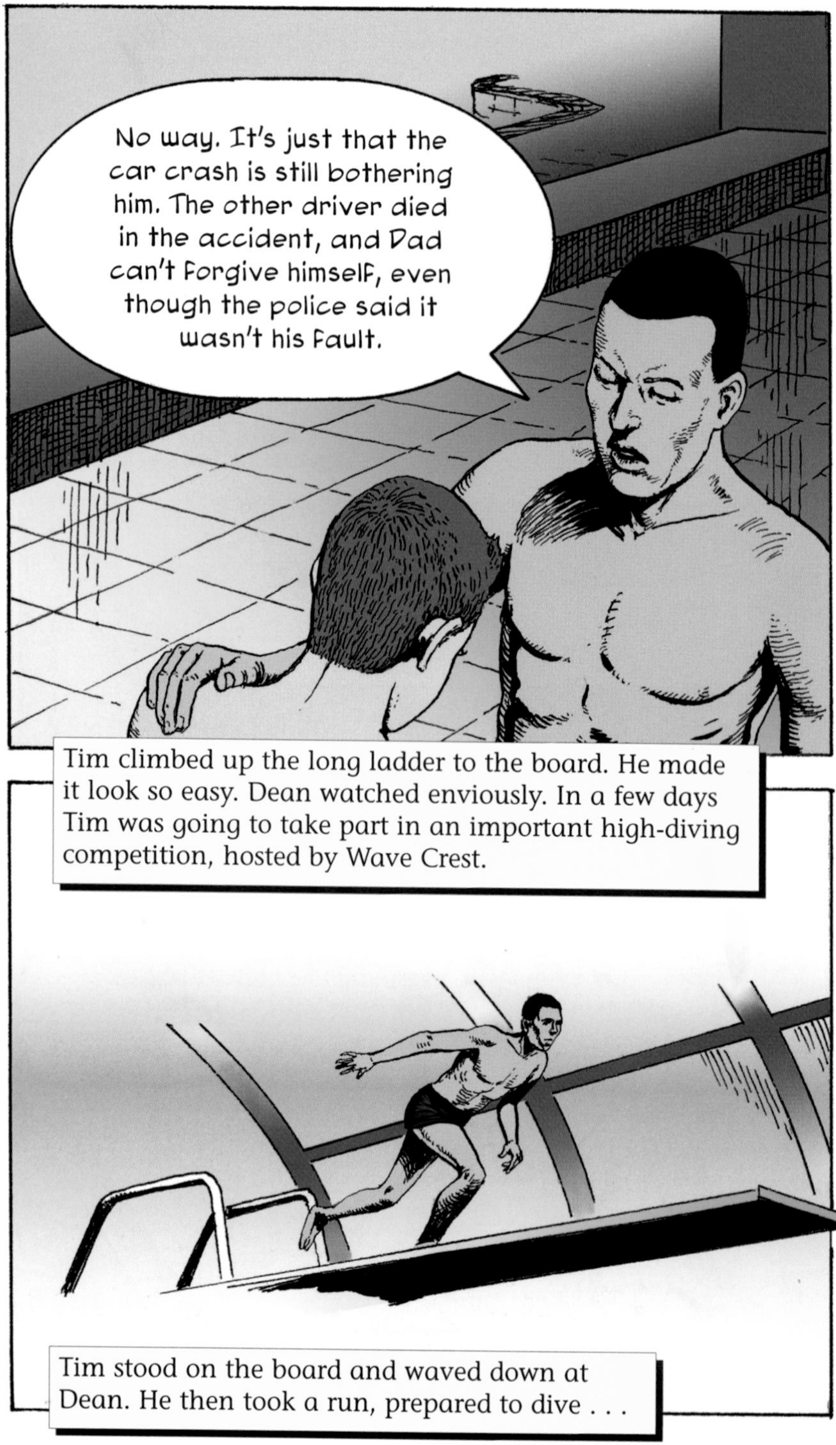
No way. It's just that the car crash is still bothering him. The other driver died in the accident, and Dad can't forgive himself, even though the police said it wasn't his fault.
Tim climbed up the long ladder to the board. He made it look so easy. Dean watched enviously. In a few days Tim was going to take part in an important high-diving competition, hosted by Wave Crest.
Tim stood on the board and waved down at Dean. He then took a run, prepared to dive . . .

. . . suddenly, the board collapsed. On his way down, Tim's ankle hit the lower diving board.

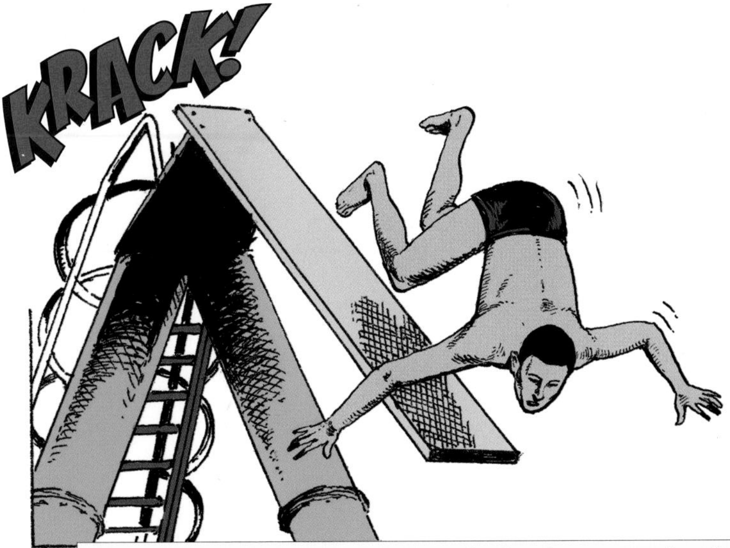
KRACK!

Without thinking, Dean jumped after him into the diving pool — even though he hated the deep water. He was a fast swimmer, and he soon reached Tim, who was floating on his back, sputtering. Tim was grinning, even though he was in pain.

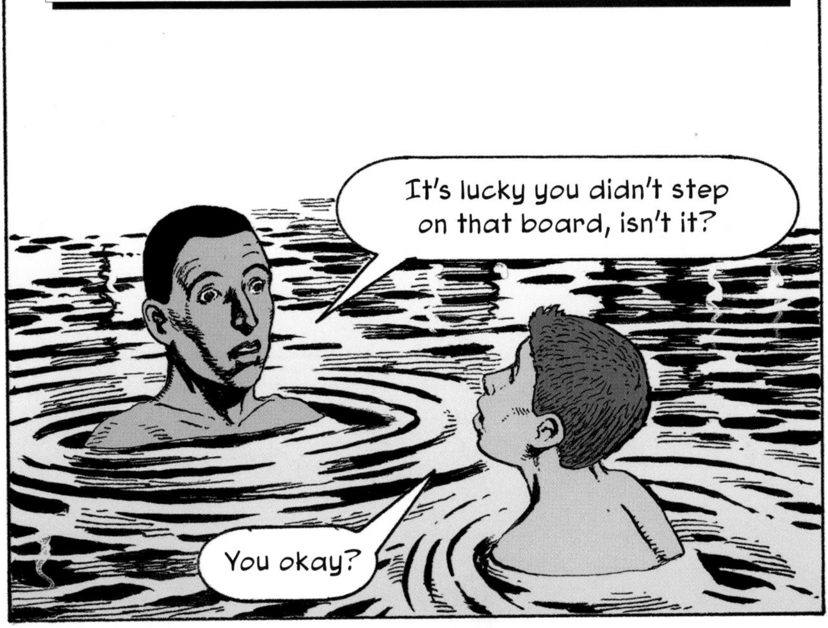
It's lucky you didn't step on that board, isn't it?
You okay?

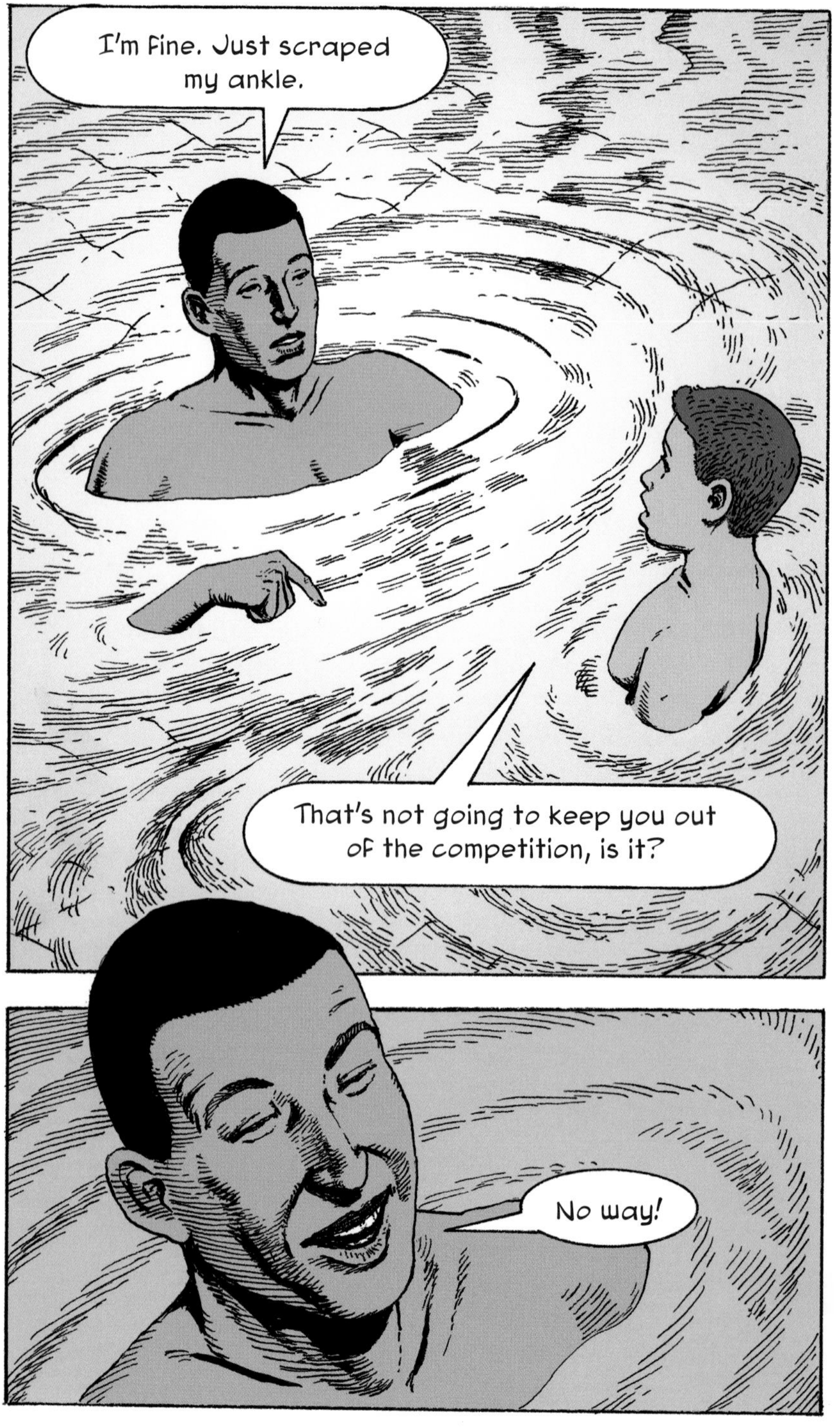
I'm fine. Just scraped my ankle.
That's not going to keep you out of the competition, is it?
No way!

Tim hauled himself up on the side of the pool, and Dean followed.

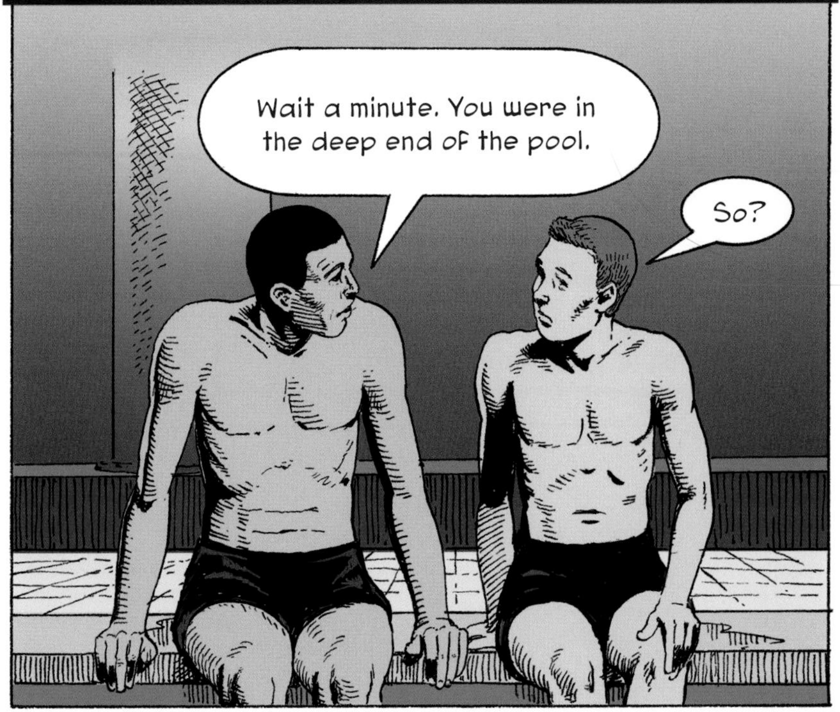
Wait a minute. You were in the deep end of the pool.
So?

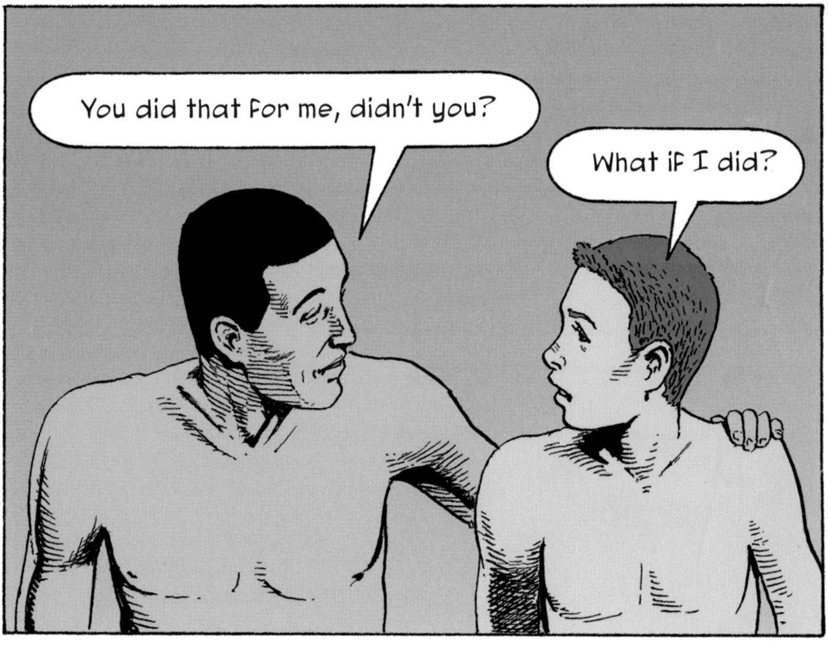
You did that for me, didn't you?
What if I did?

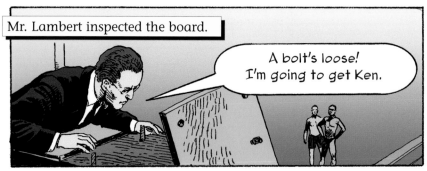

Mr. Lambert inspected the board.

A bolt's loose! I'm going to get Ken.

He went off to find Ken Drake, the club's building engineer, as well as the swimming coach.

That's weird, isn't it? Ken inspects all the equipment every day. How could he miss that?

Maybe the bolt slowly worked loose.

Something bad is going on.

CHAPTER TWO

The next day, Ken and Mr. Lambert were coaching some of the young divers, including Ben Robinson, Tim's closest rival.

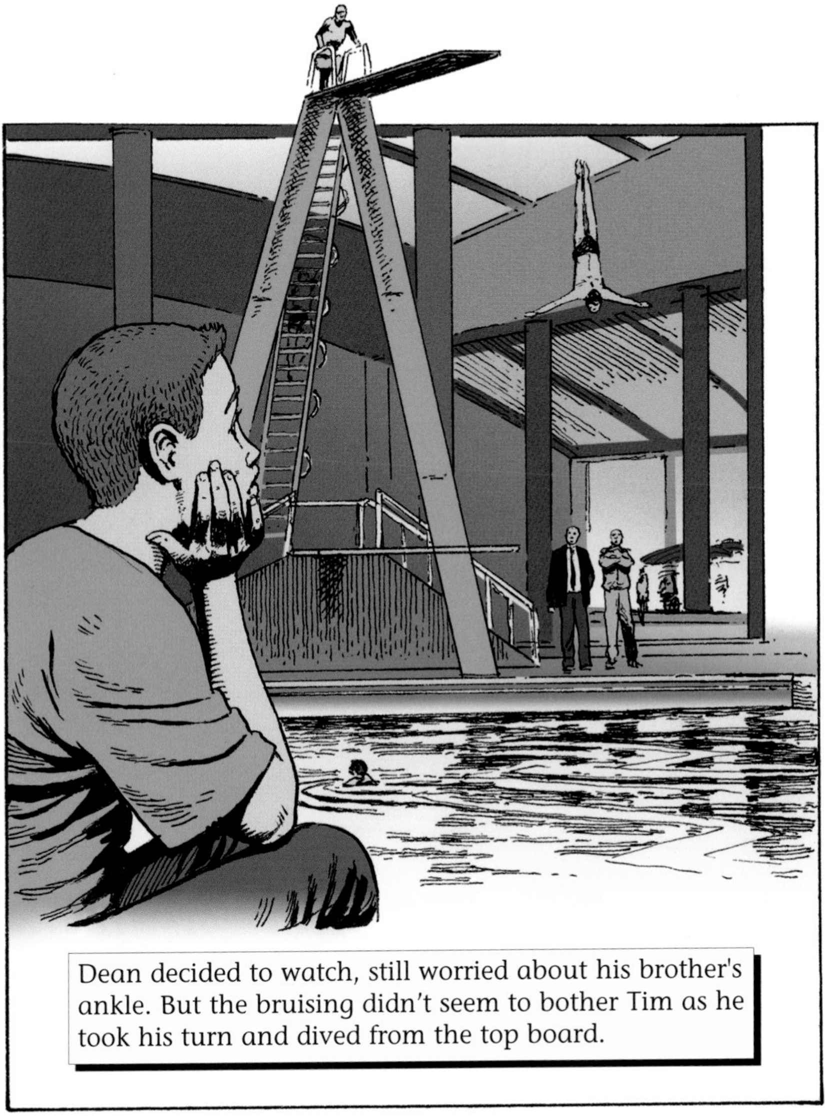
Dean decided to watch, still worried about his brother's ankle. But the bruising didn't seem to bother Tim as he took his turn and dived from the top board.

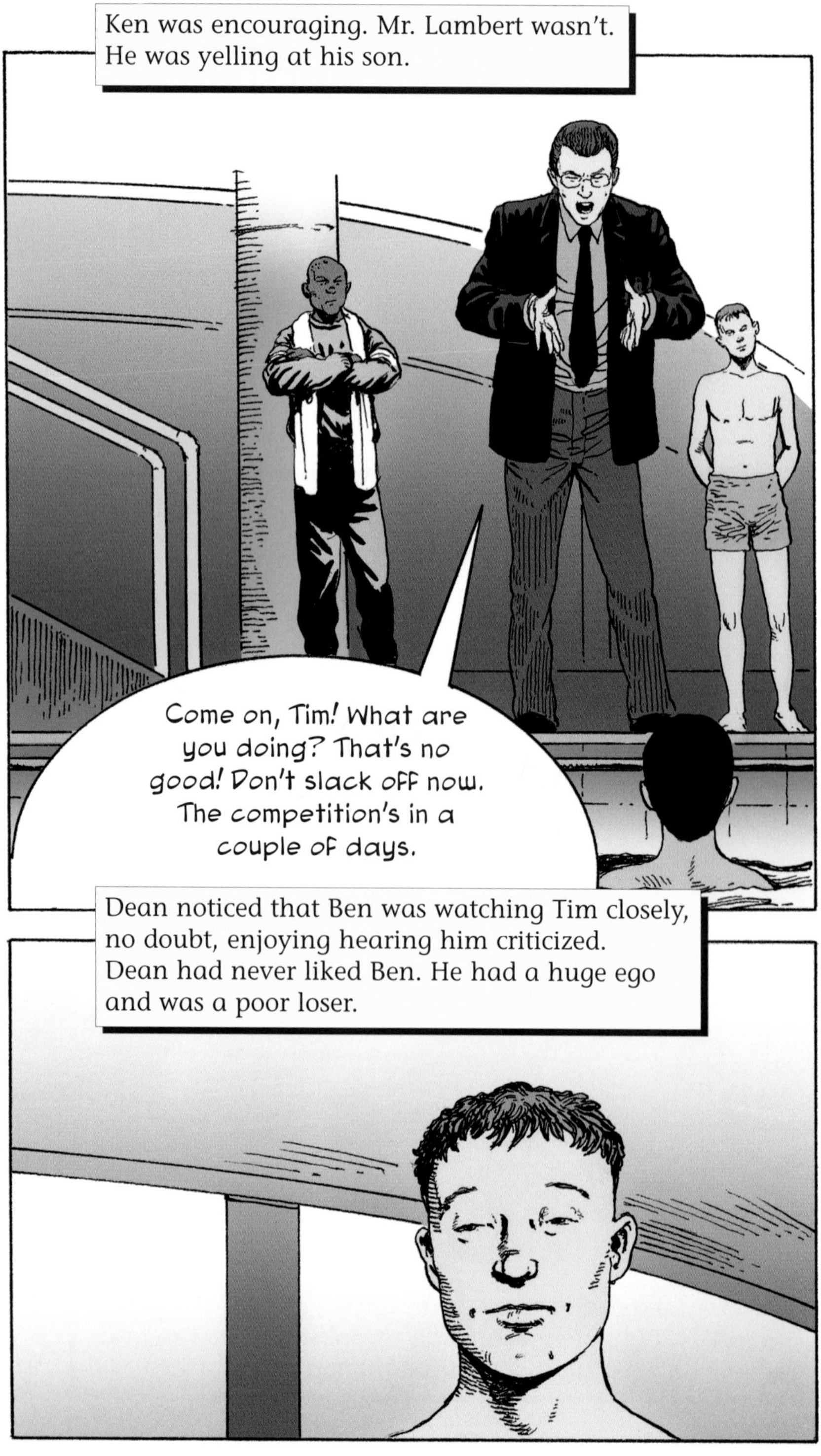
Ken was encouraging. Mr. Lambert wasn't. He was yelling at his son.
Come on, Tim! What are you doing? That's no good! Don't slack off now. The competition's in a couple of days.
Dean noticed that Ben was watching Tim closely, no doubt, enjoying hearing him criticized. Dean had never liked Ben. He had a huge ego and was a poor loser.

At the end of the practice, Dean was even more worried as he overheard a fight between his dad and Ken. They were shouting at each other so loudly it was impossible not to hear them.

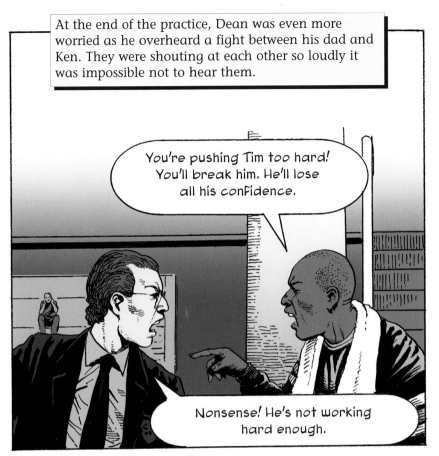

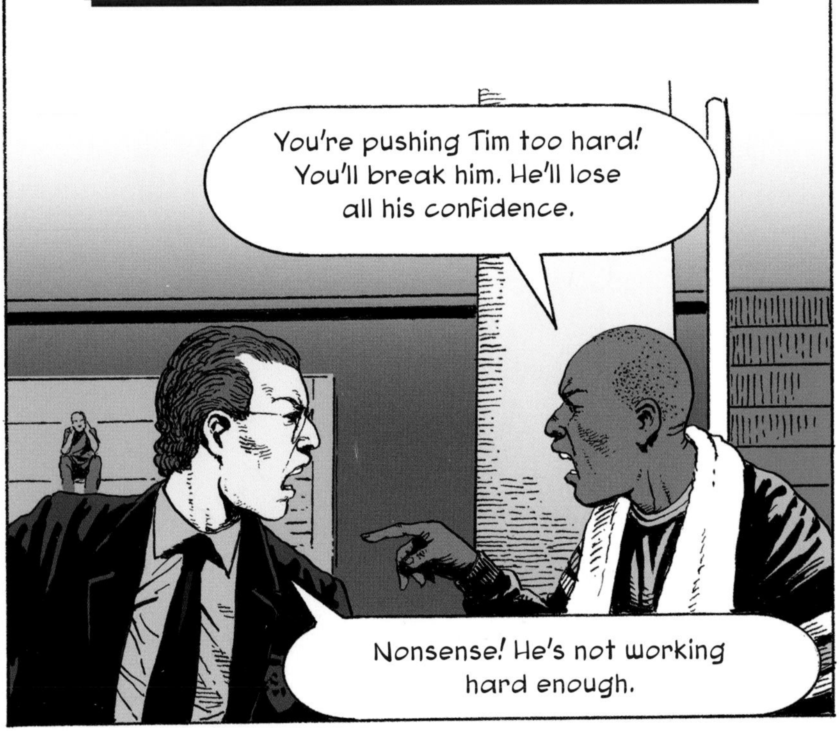
You're pushing Tim too hard! You'll break him. He'll lose all his confidence.
Nonsense! He's not working hard enough.

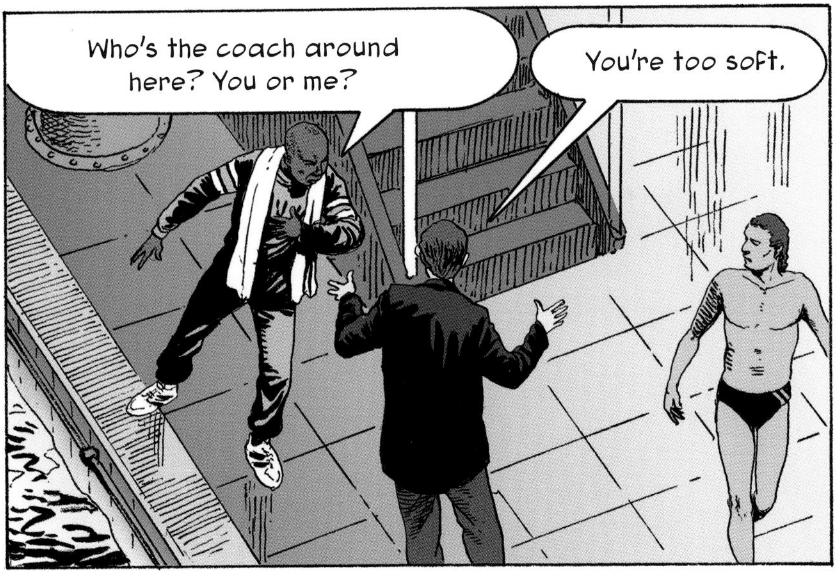
Who's the coach around here? You or me?
You're too soft.

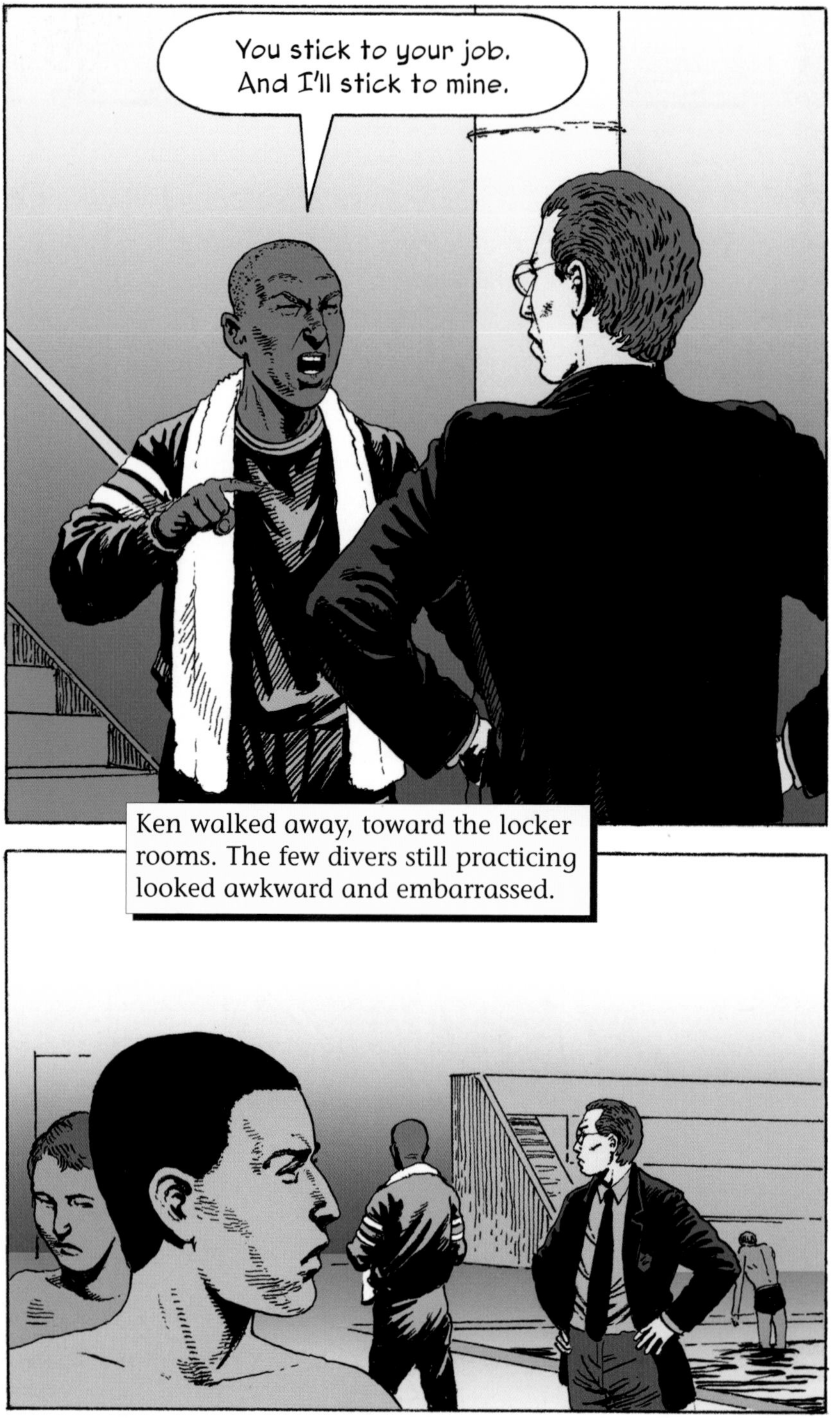
You stick to your job. And I'll stick to mine.
Ken walked away, toward the locker rooms. The few divers still practicing looked awkward and embarrassed.

CHAPTER THREE

A poolside dance that evening celebrated the opening of Raging Waters, the new water slides at the health club. Swimmers entered the three slides, plunged through twisting tubes on streams of water, and tumbled into a pool at the bottom.

Tim and Dean went with Maggie and Dawn, two of the Wave Crest lifeguards.

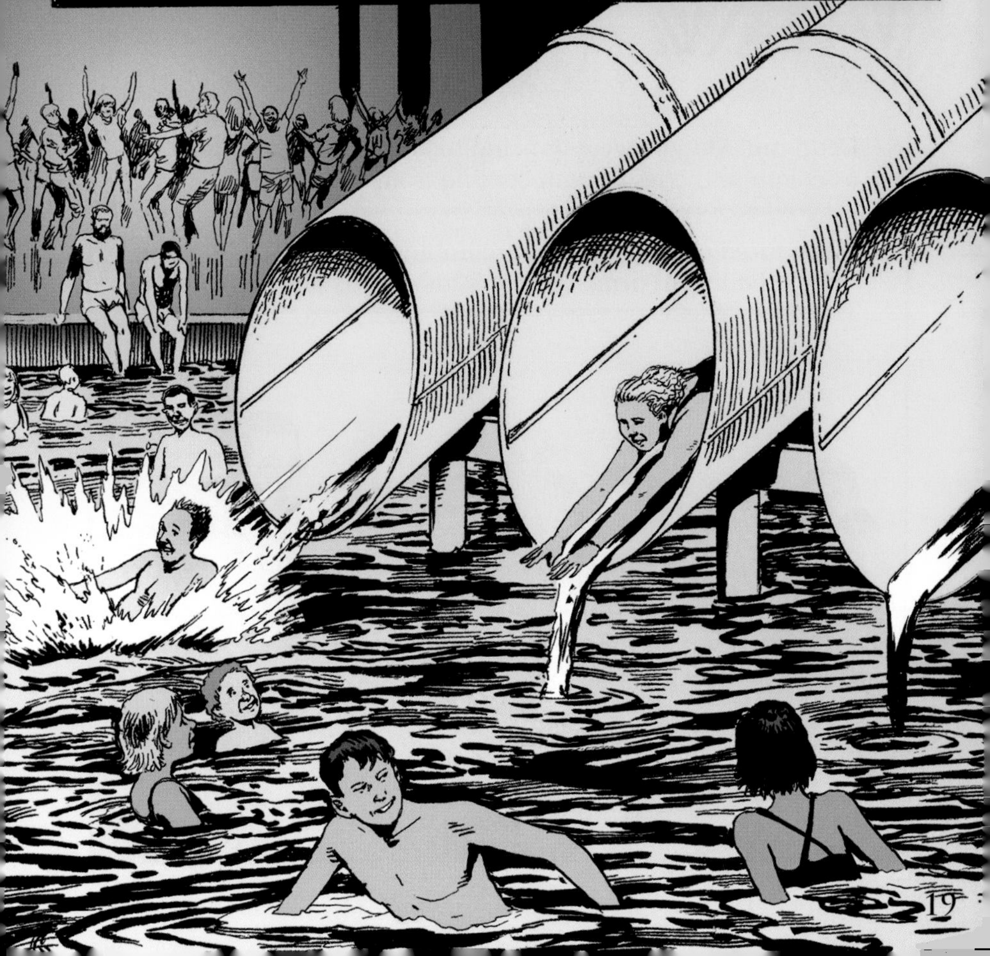

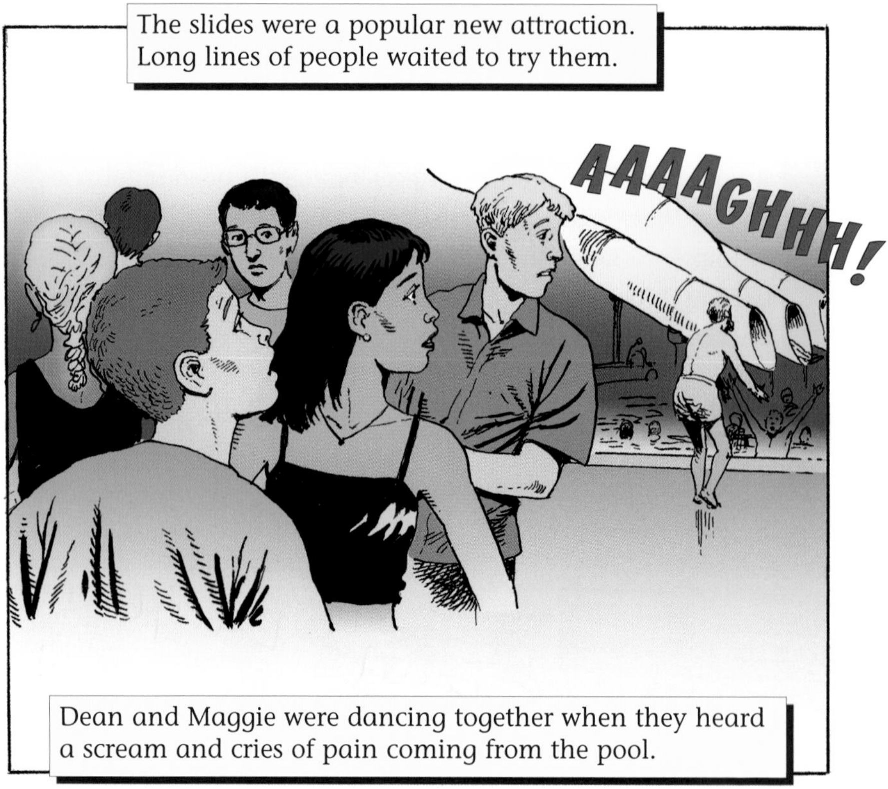
The slides were a popular new attraction. Long lines of people waited to try them.
AAAAGHHHH!
Dean and Maggie were dancing together when they heard a scream and cries of pain coming from the pool.

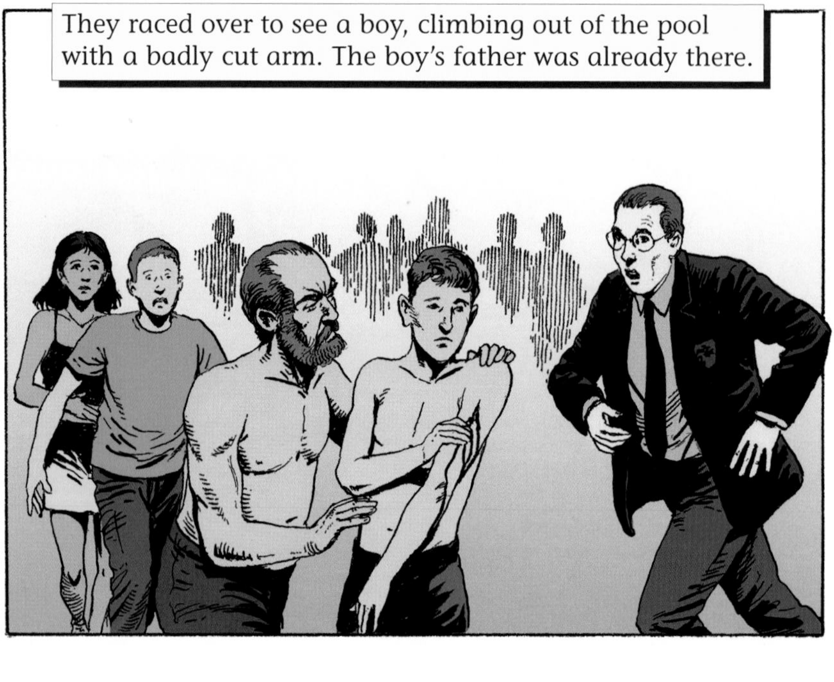
They raced over to see a boy, climbing out of the pool with a badly cut arm. The boy's father was already there.

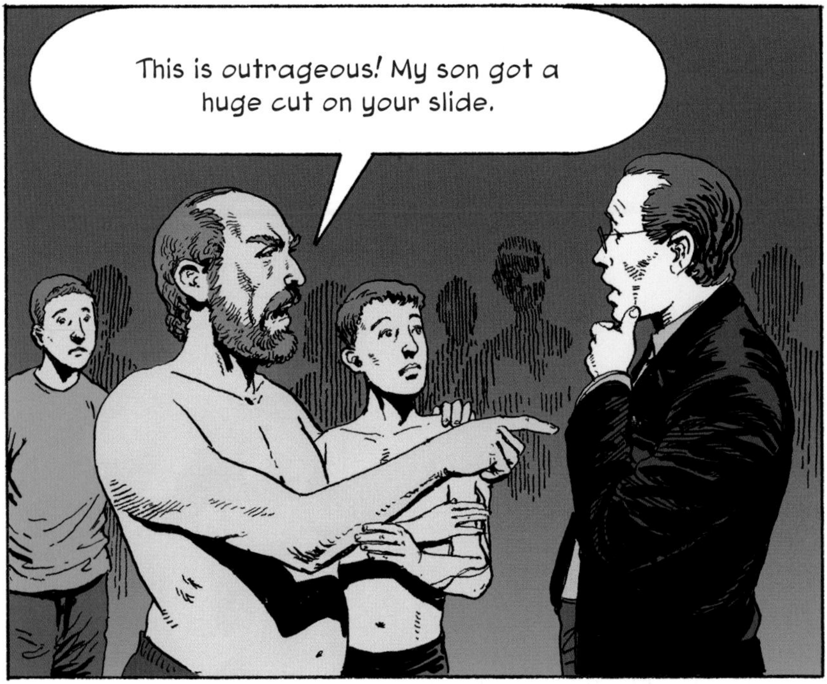
This is outrageous! My son got a huge cut on your slide.

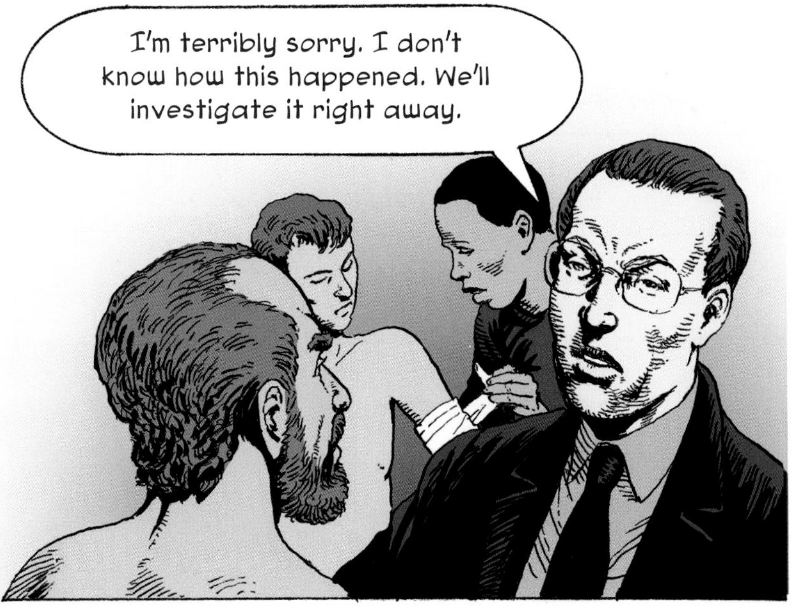
I'm terribly sorry. I don't know how this happened. We'll investigate it right away.

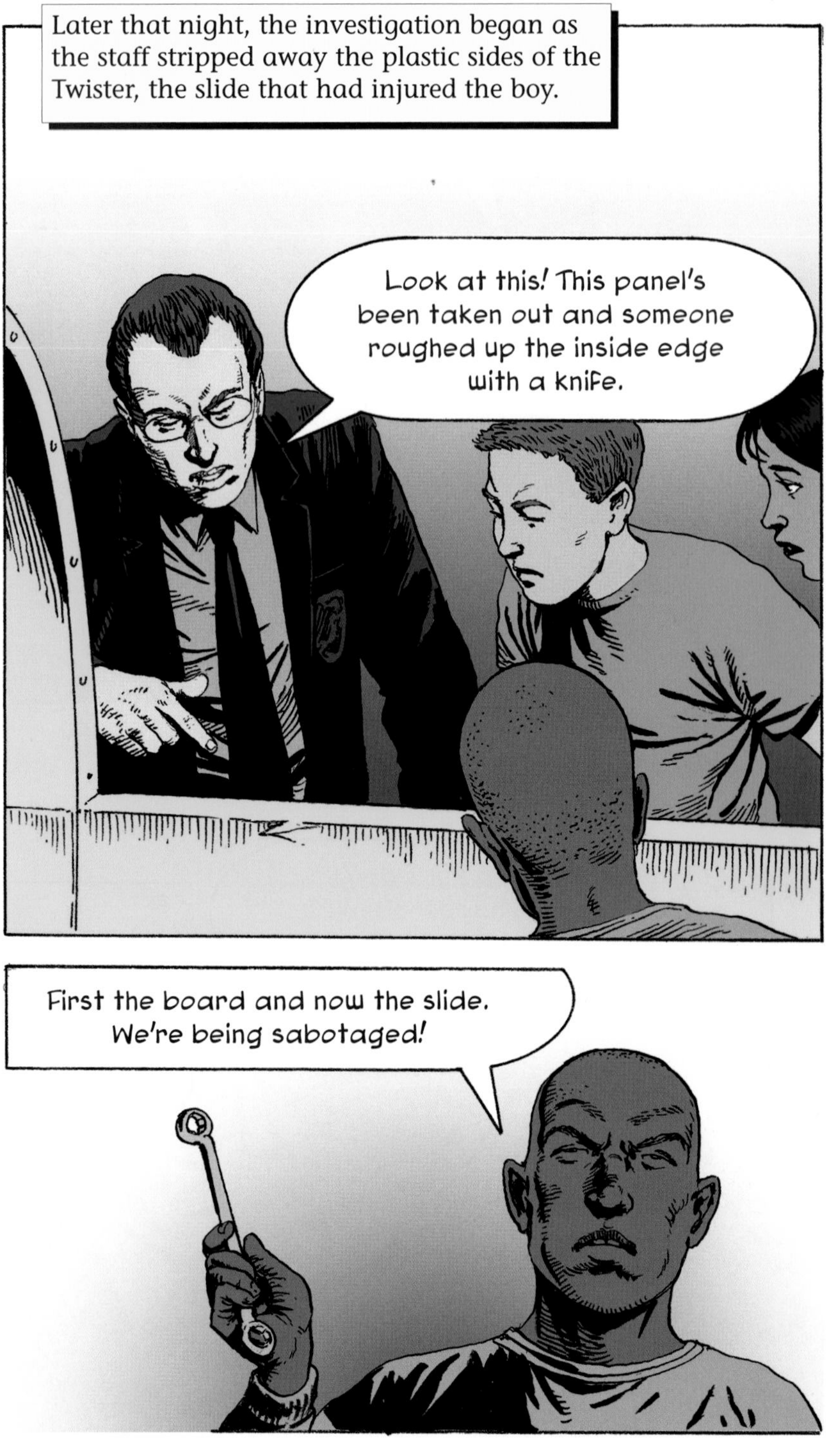
Later that night, the investigation began as the staff stripped away the plastic sides of the Twister, the slide that had injured the boy.
Look at this! This panel's been taken out and someone roughed up the inside edge with a knife.
First the board and now the slide. We're being sabotaged!

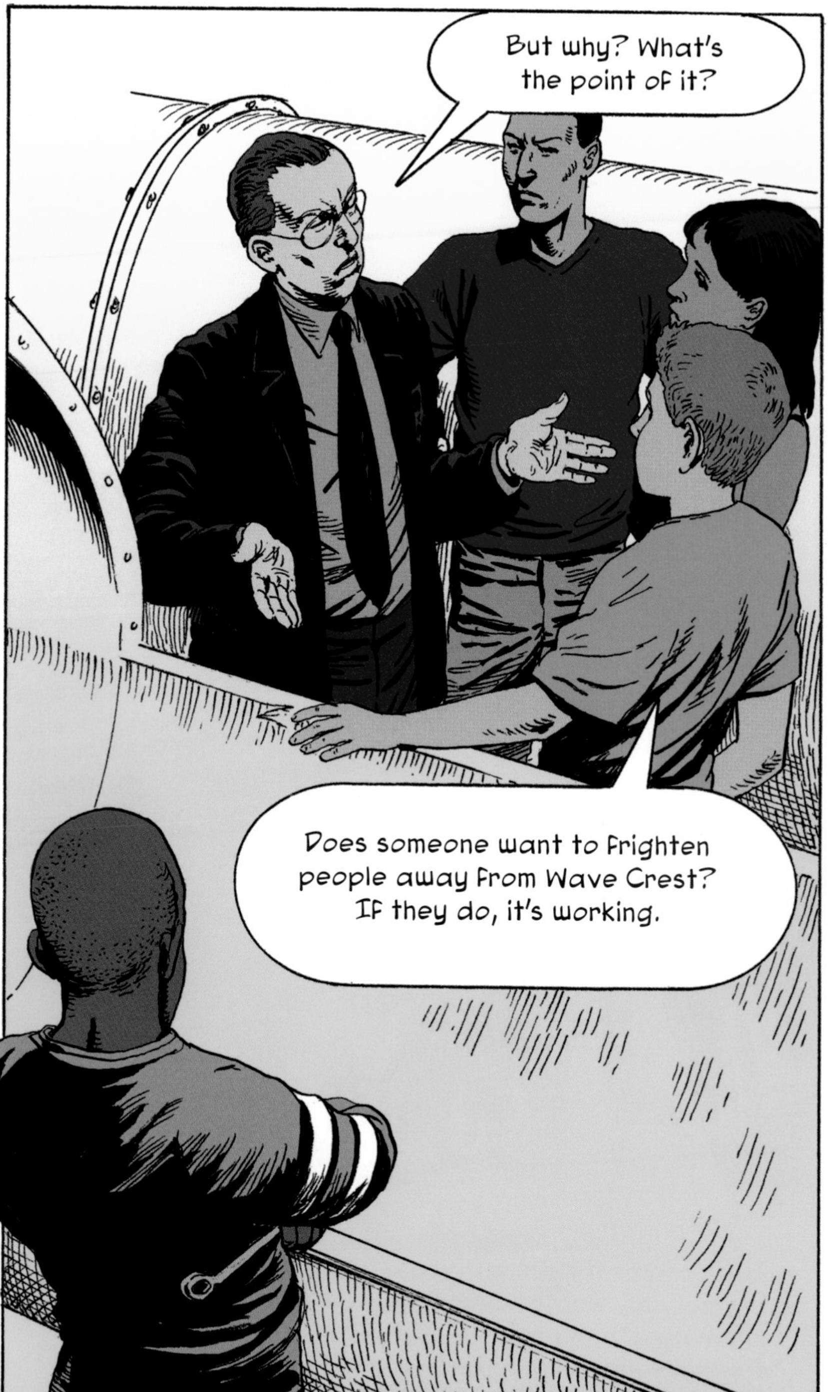
But why? What's the point of it?
Does someone want to frighten people away from Wave Crest? If they do, it's working.

Afterwards, Dean and Maggie walked home through the dark winter streets. Dean liked Maggie a lot. She was funny and cute, and she seemed to like him, too. She was his first regular girlfriend.

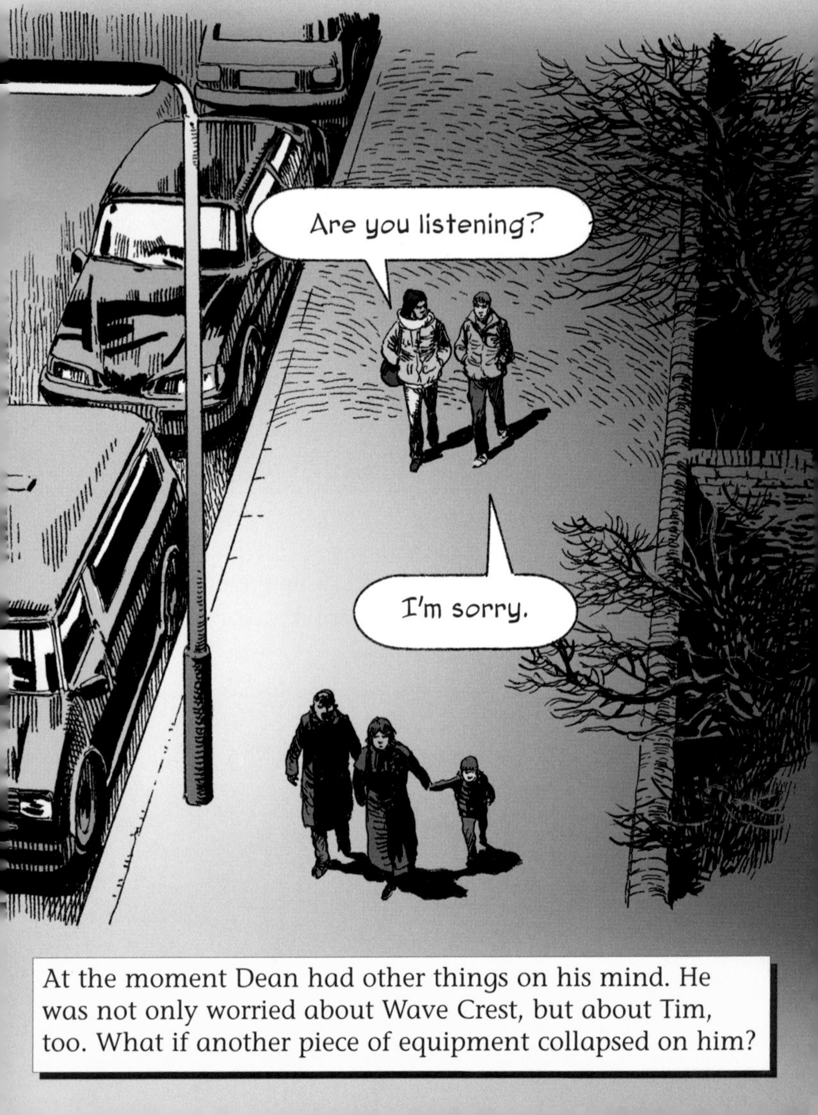
Are you listening?
I'm sorry.

At the moment Dean had other things on his mind. He was not only worried about Wave Crest, but about Tim, too. What if another piece of equipment collapsed on him?

Then there was his dad to consider. He'd been so quiet since the car crash, but also mean and bad-tempered. These accidents at Wave Crest weren't going to bring back the old Dad, who was kind and generous and fun to be with.

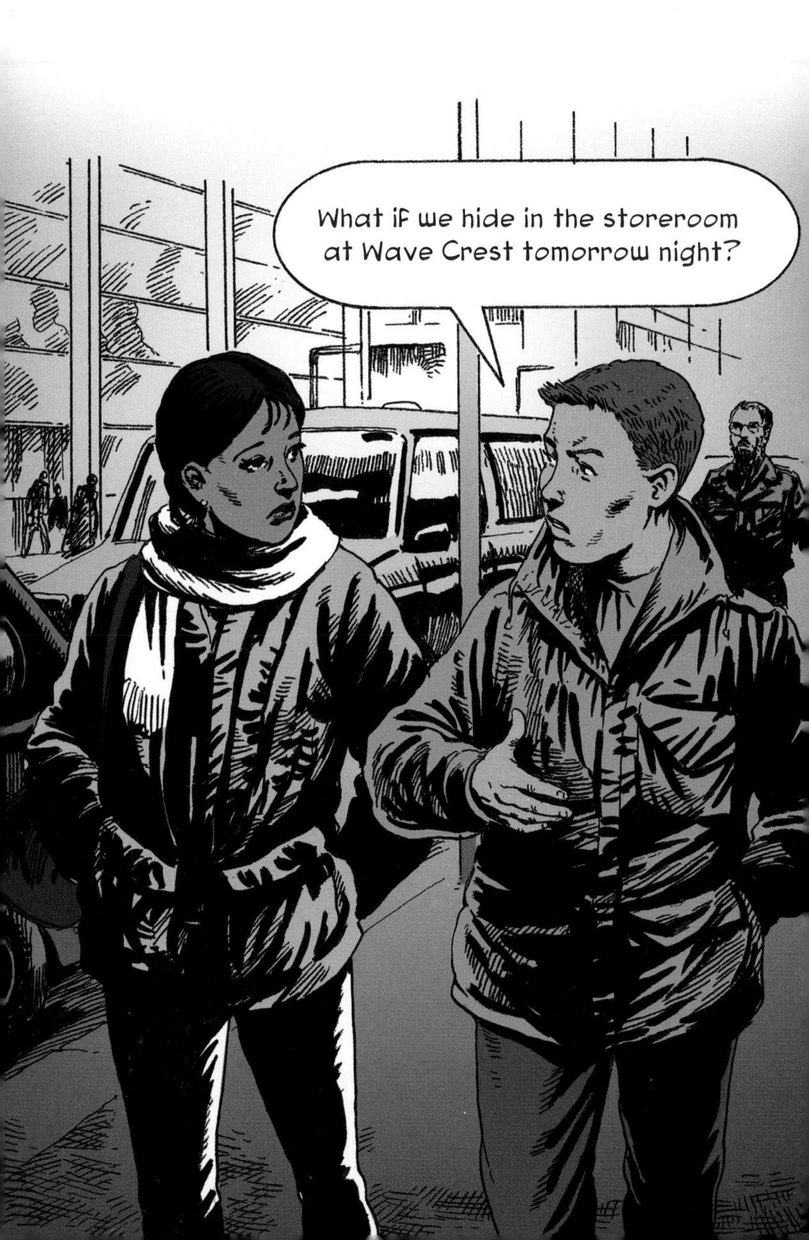
What if we hide in the storeroom at Wave Crest tomorrow night?

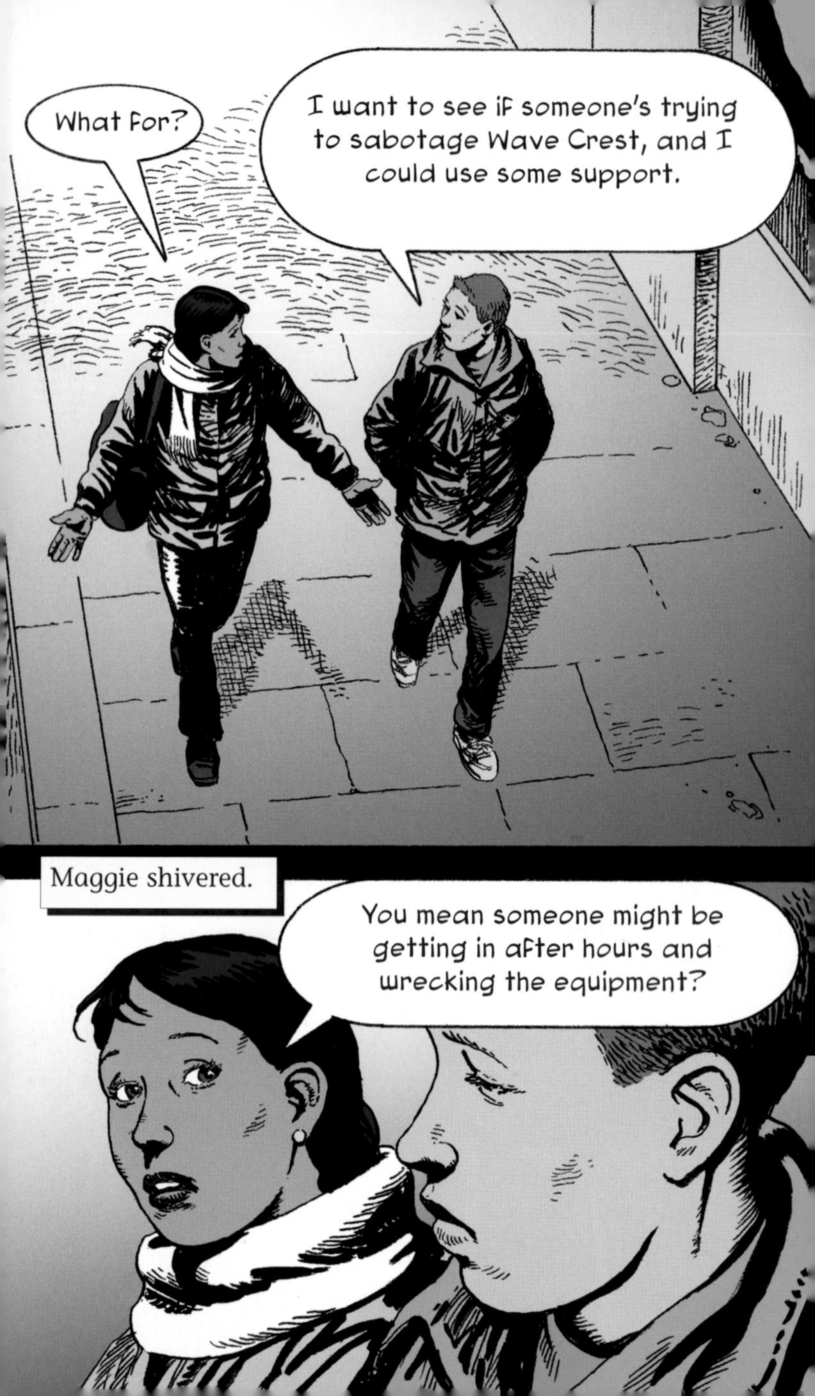
What for?
I want to see if someone's trying to sabotage Wave Crest, and I could use some support.
Maggie shivered.
You mean someone might be getting in after hours and wrecking the equipment?

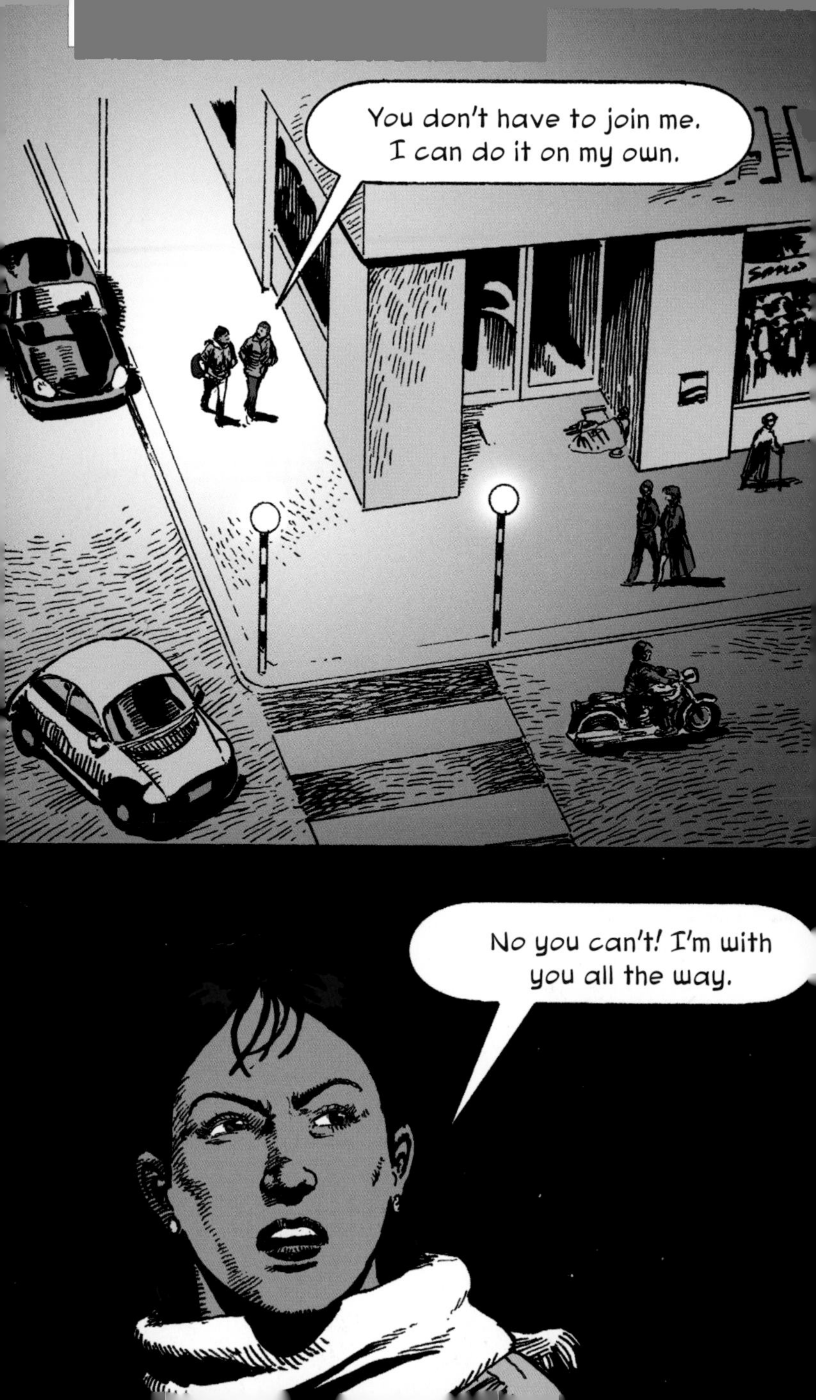
You don't have to join me. I can do it on my own.
No you can't! I'm with you all the way.

CHAPTER FOUR

The health club was eerie without its customers. All Dean and Maggie could hear from their hiding place in the storeroom the next night was the clanking of the air-vents and the gurgling of water in the pools. Maggie grabbed Dean's shoulder.

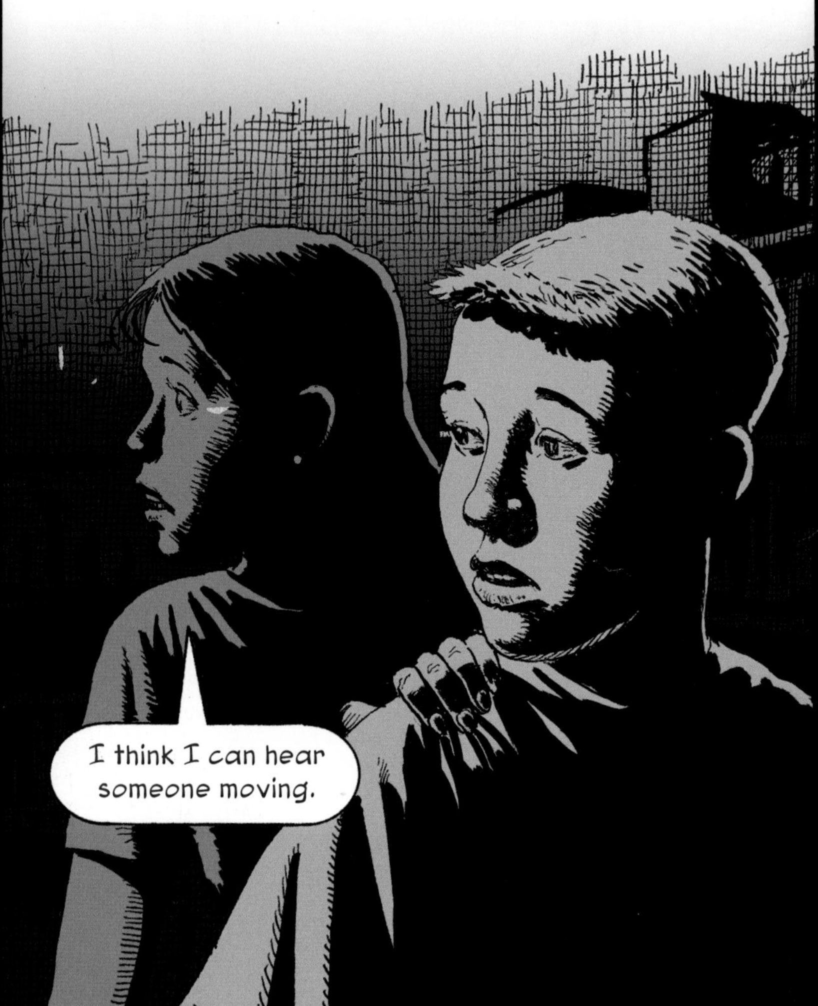
I think I can hear someone moving.

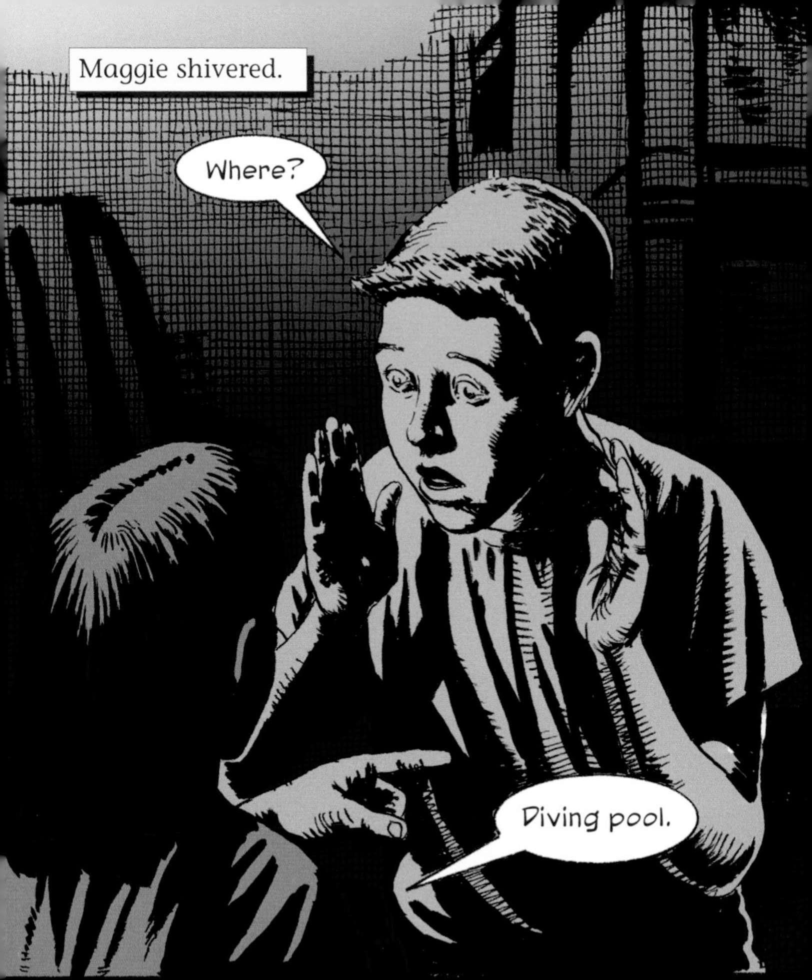
Maggie shivered.
Where?
Diving pool.
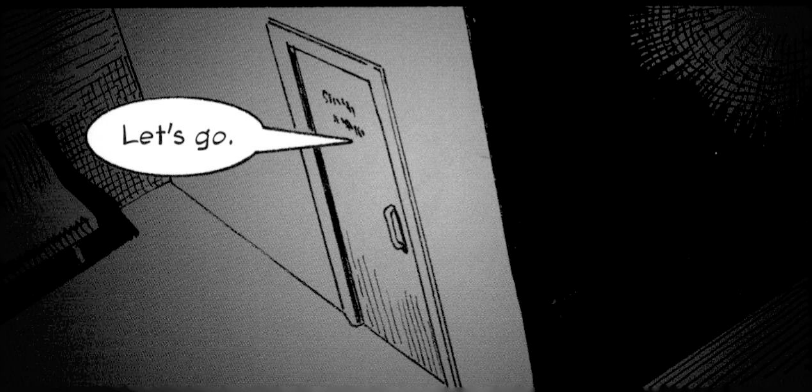
Let's go.

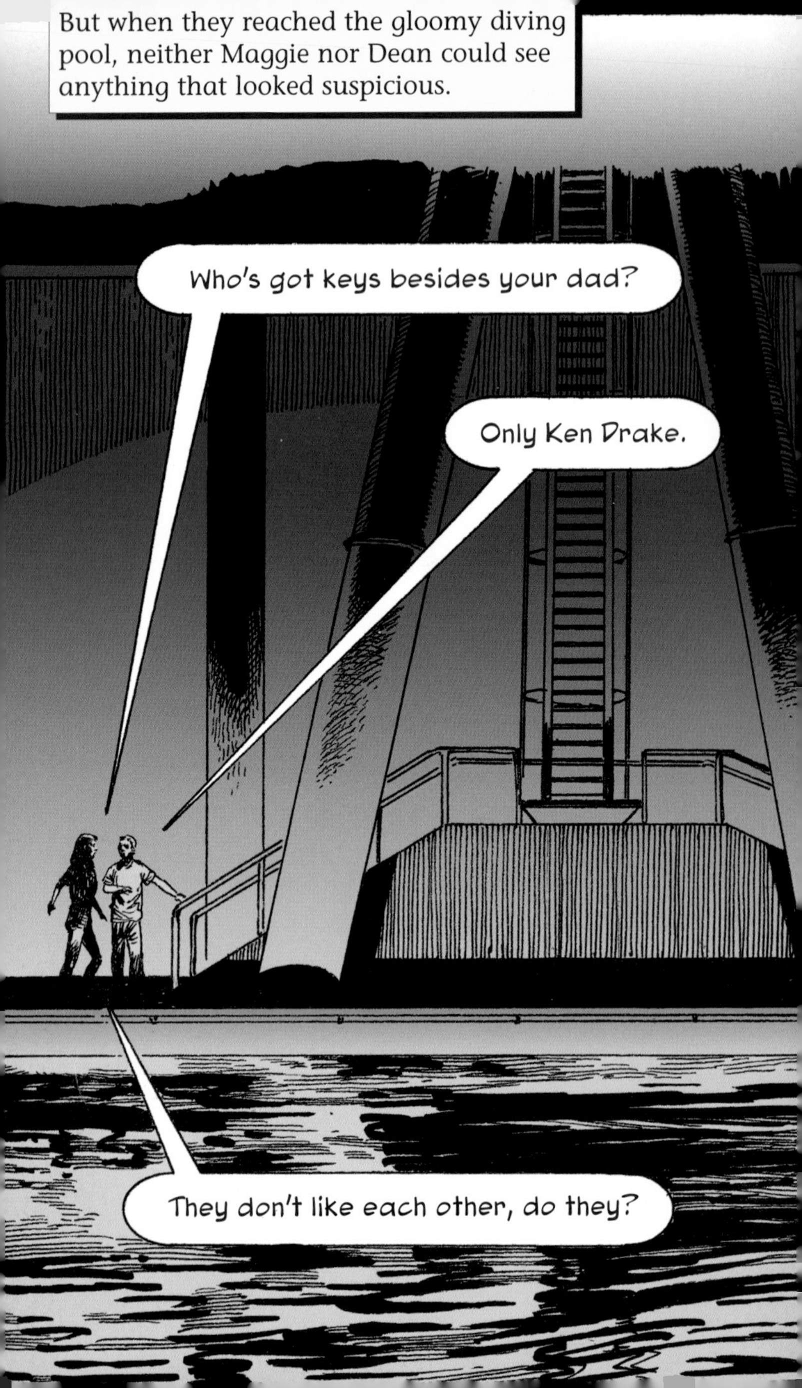
But when they reached the gloomy diving pool, neither Maggie nor Dean could see anything that looked suspicious.
Who's got keys besides your dad?
Only Ken Drake.
They don't like each other, do they?

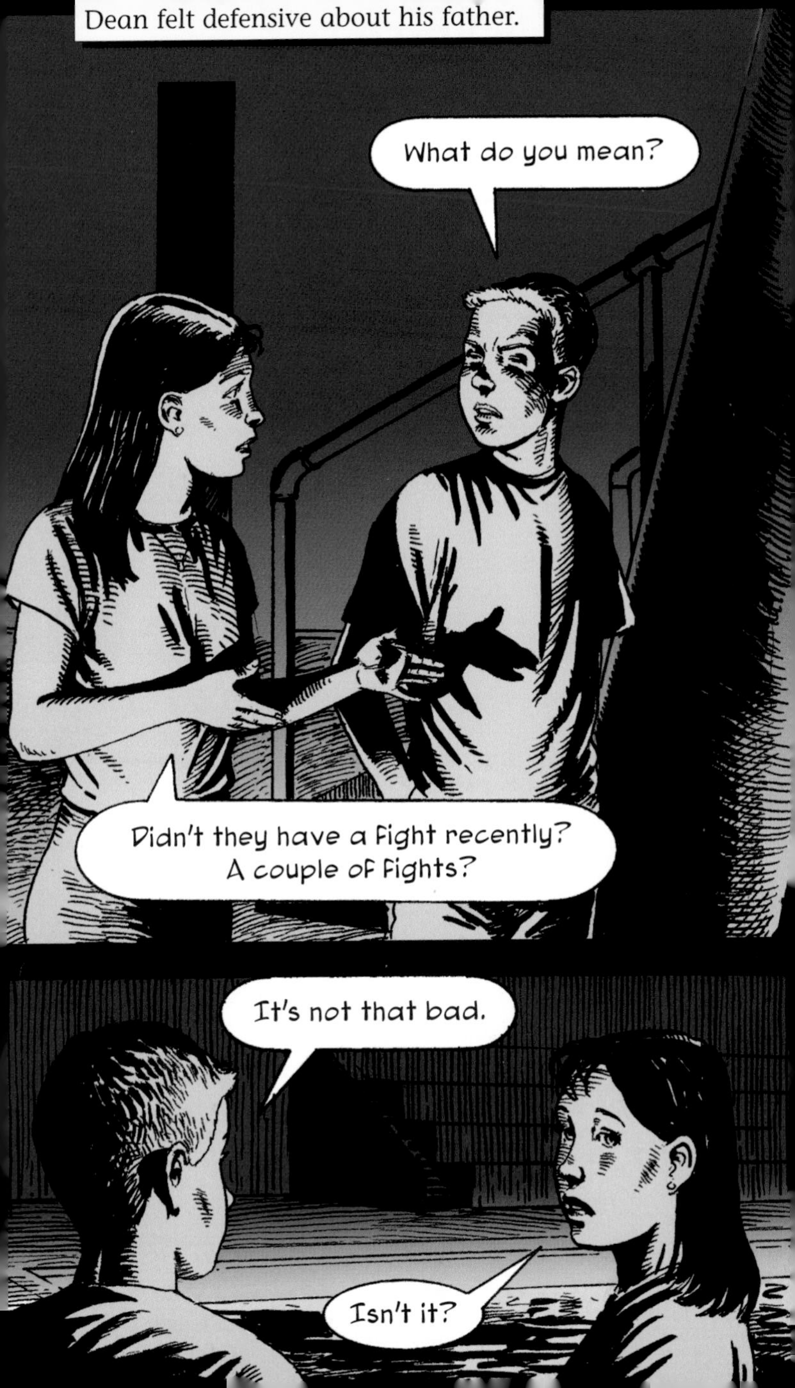
Dean felt defensive about his father.
What do you mean?
Didn't they have a fight recently? A couple of fights?
It's not that bad.
Isn't it?

CHAPTER FIVE

The next day, Mr. Lambert was furious when he heard a rumor about what Dean and Maggie had done last night.

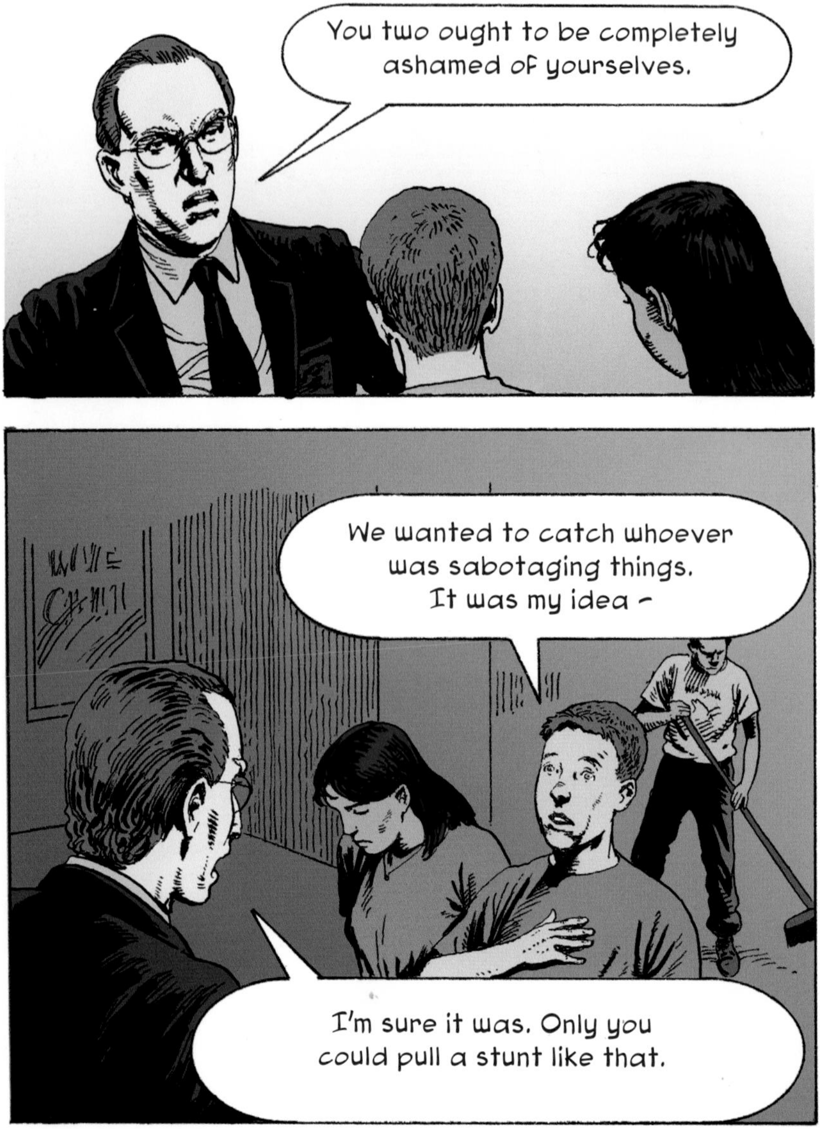
You two ought to be completely ashamed of yourselves.
We wanted to catch whoever was sabotaging things. It was my idea -
I'm sure it was. Only you could pull a stunt like that.

That evening a large audience sat around the pool as the divers awaited the beginning of the competition. Dean and Maggie had good seats next to the high-diving board. On the opposite side were Mr. Lambert and Ken Drake, near the row of judges. All of the divers' friends and families were there.

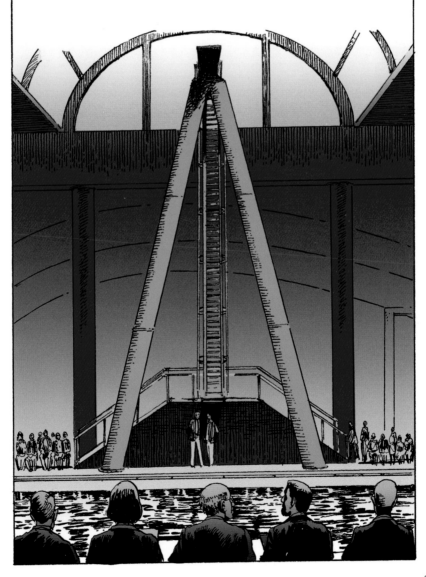

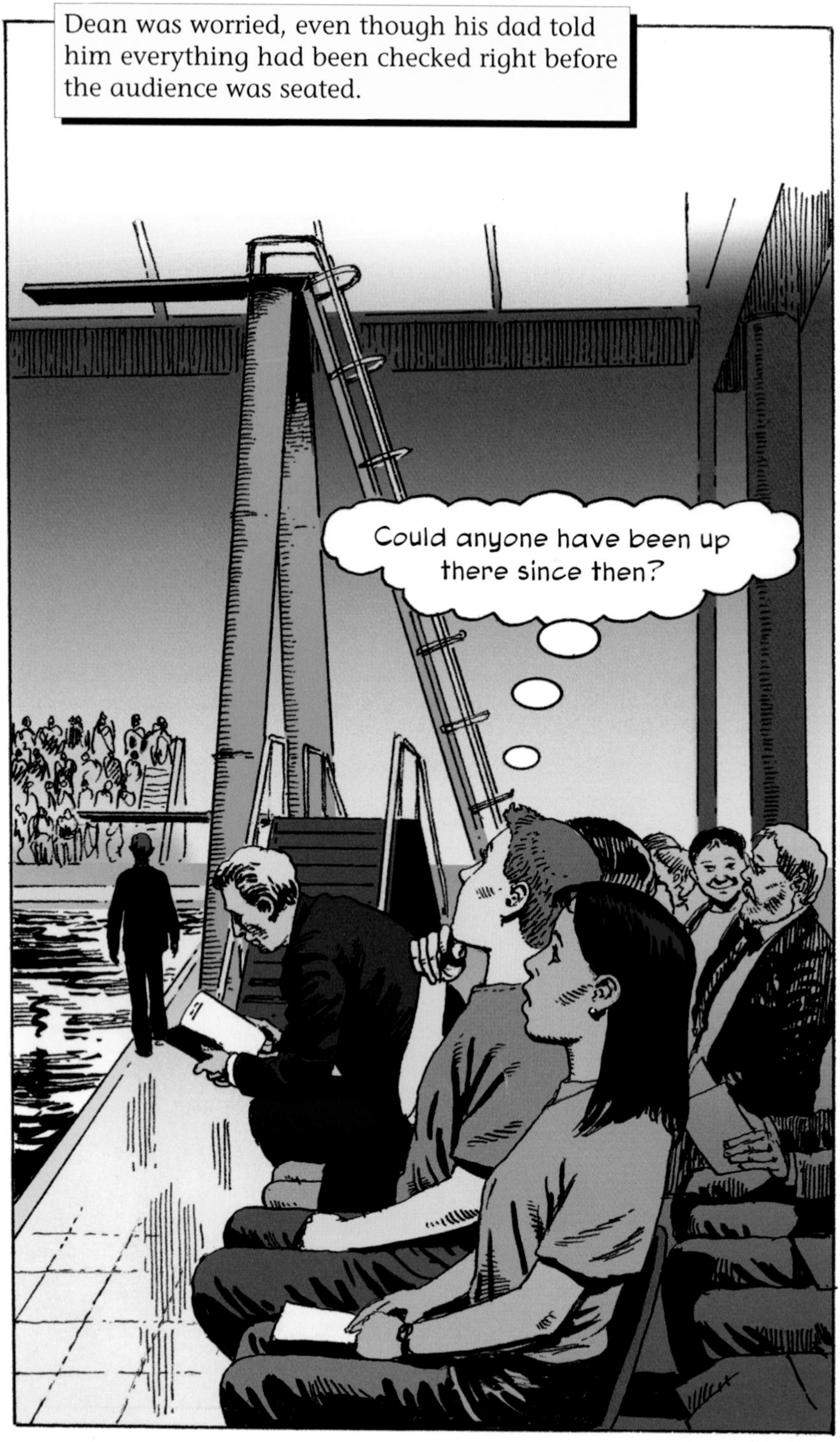
Dean was worried, even though his dad told him everything had been checked right before the audience was seated.
Could anyone have been up there since then?

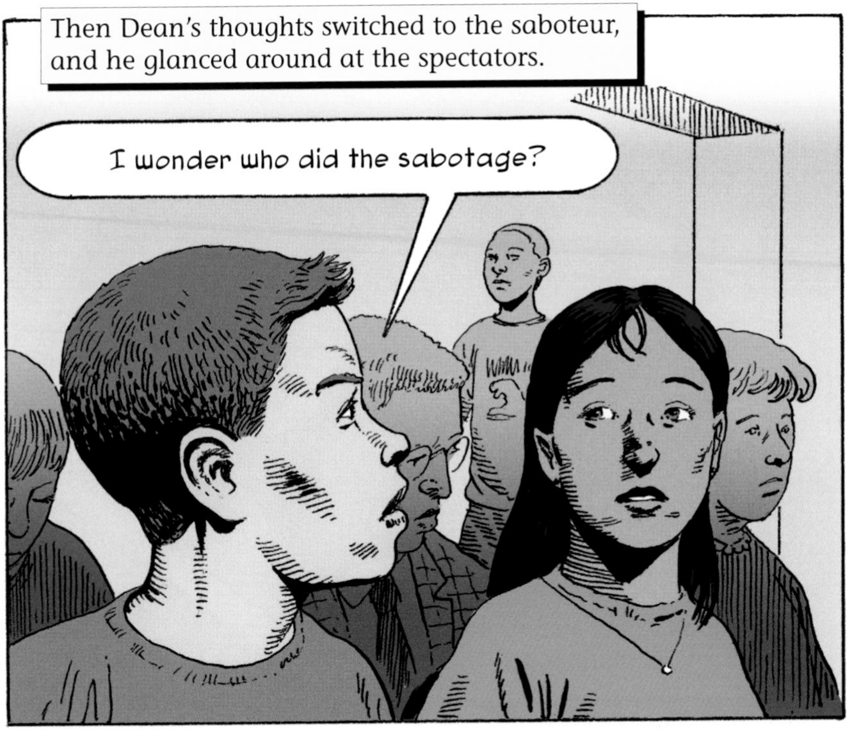

Then Dean's thoughts switched to the saboteur, and he glanced around at the spectators.
I wonder who did the sabotage?

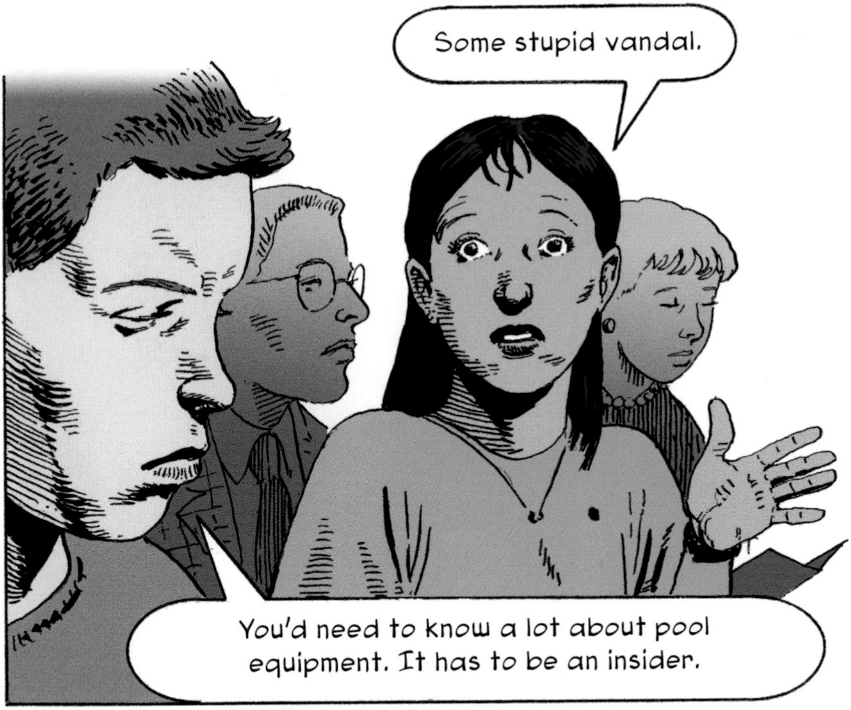

Some stupid vandal.
You'd need to know a lot about pool equipment. It has to be an insider.

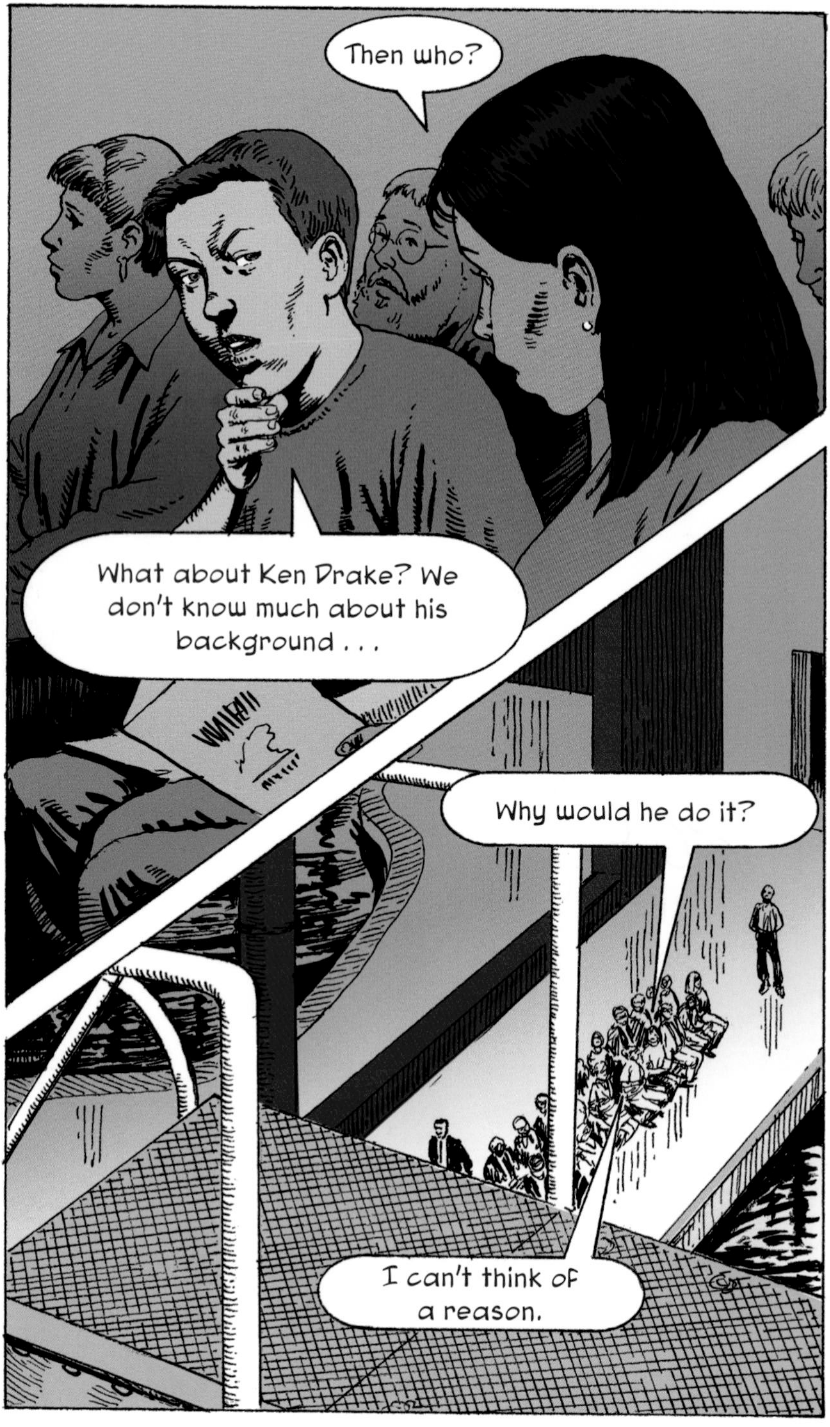
Then who?
What about Ken Drake? We don't know much about his background . . .
Why would he do it?
I can't think of a reason.

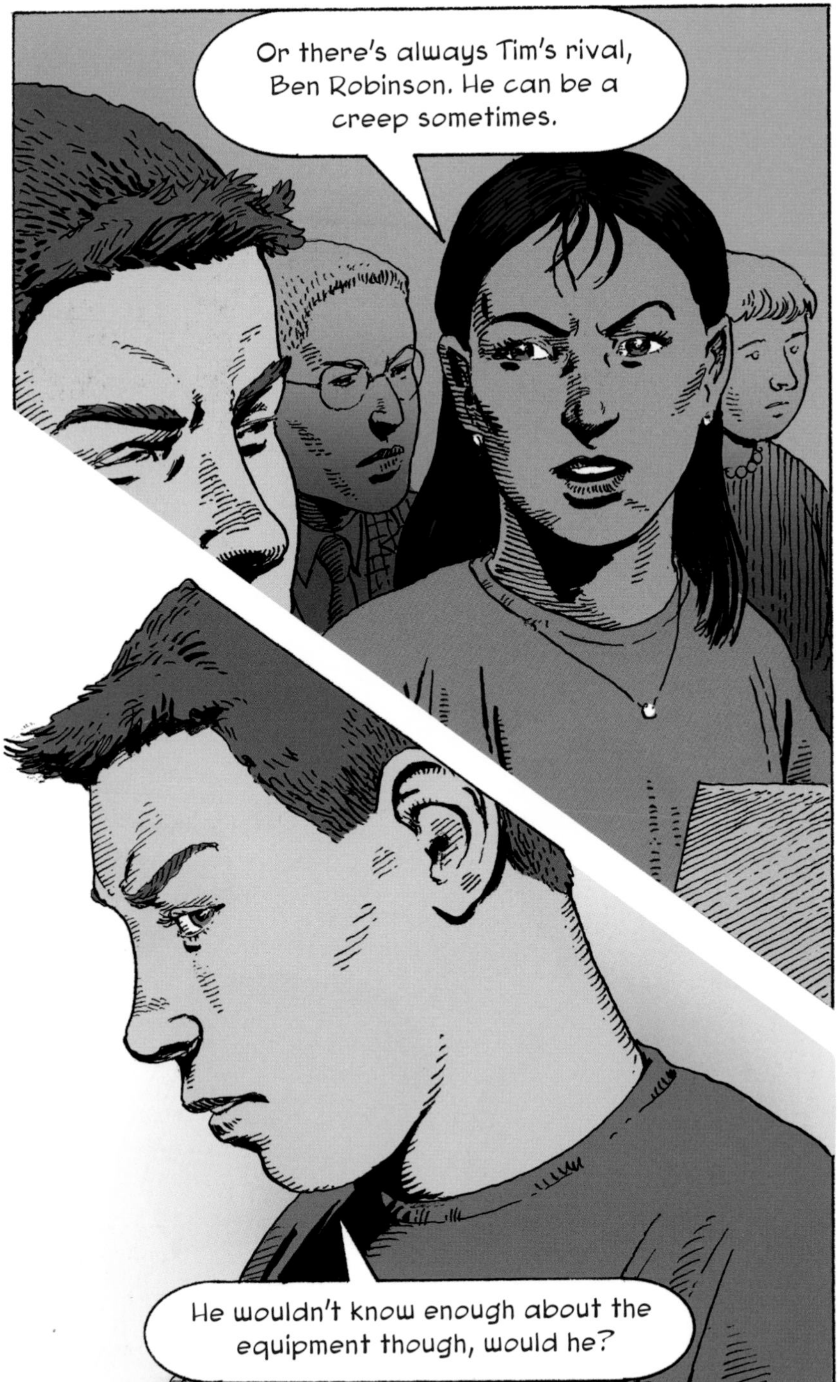
Or there's always Tim's rival, Ben Robinson. He can be a creep sometimes.
He wouldn't know enough about the equipment though, would he?

Dawn passed by. Dean leaned over and whispered to her.

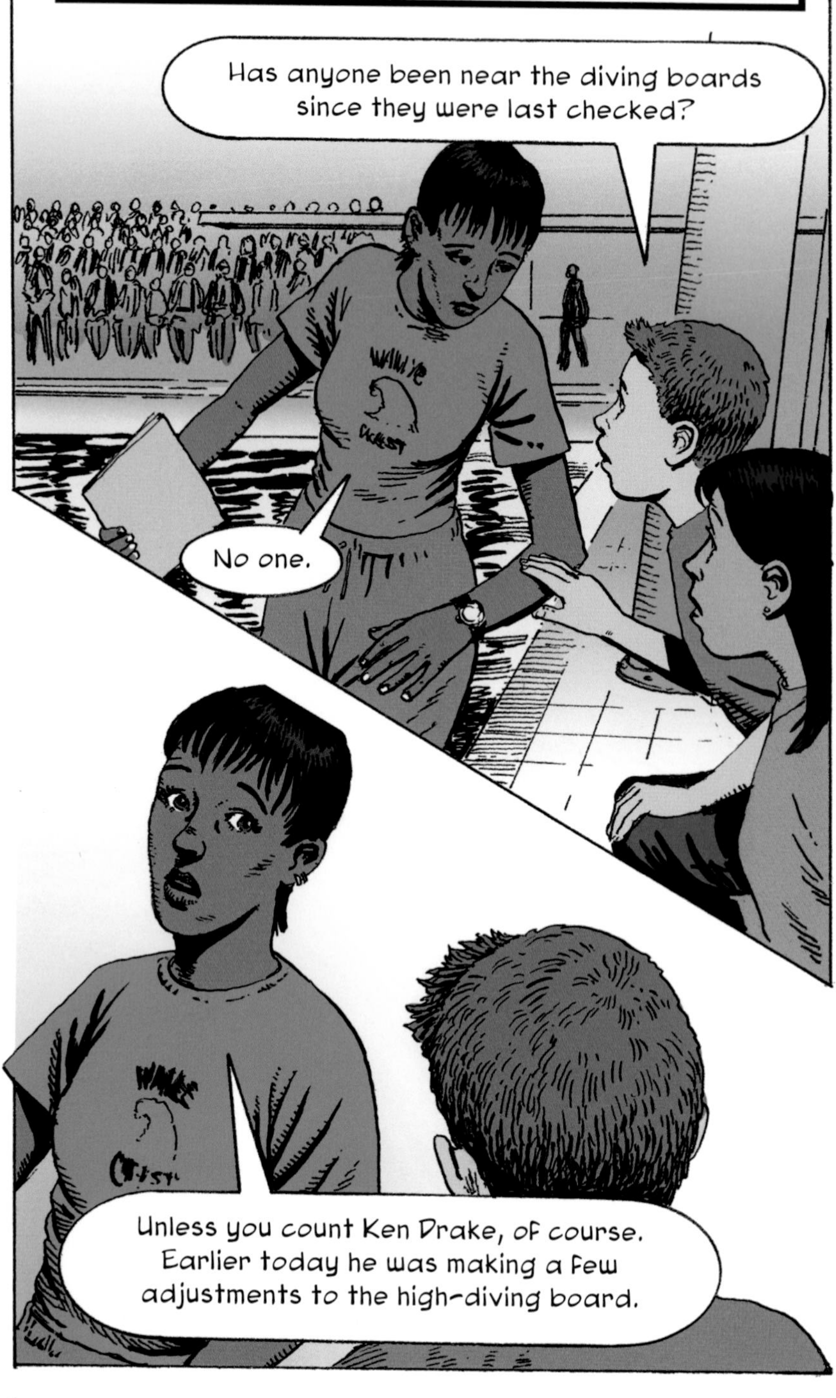
Has anyone been near the diving boards since they were last checked?
No one.
Unless you count Ken Drake, of course. Earlier today he was making a few adjustments to the high-diving board.

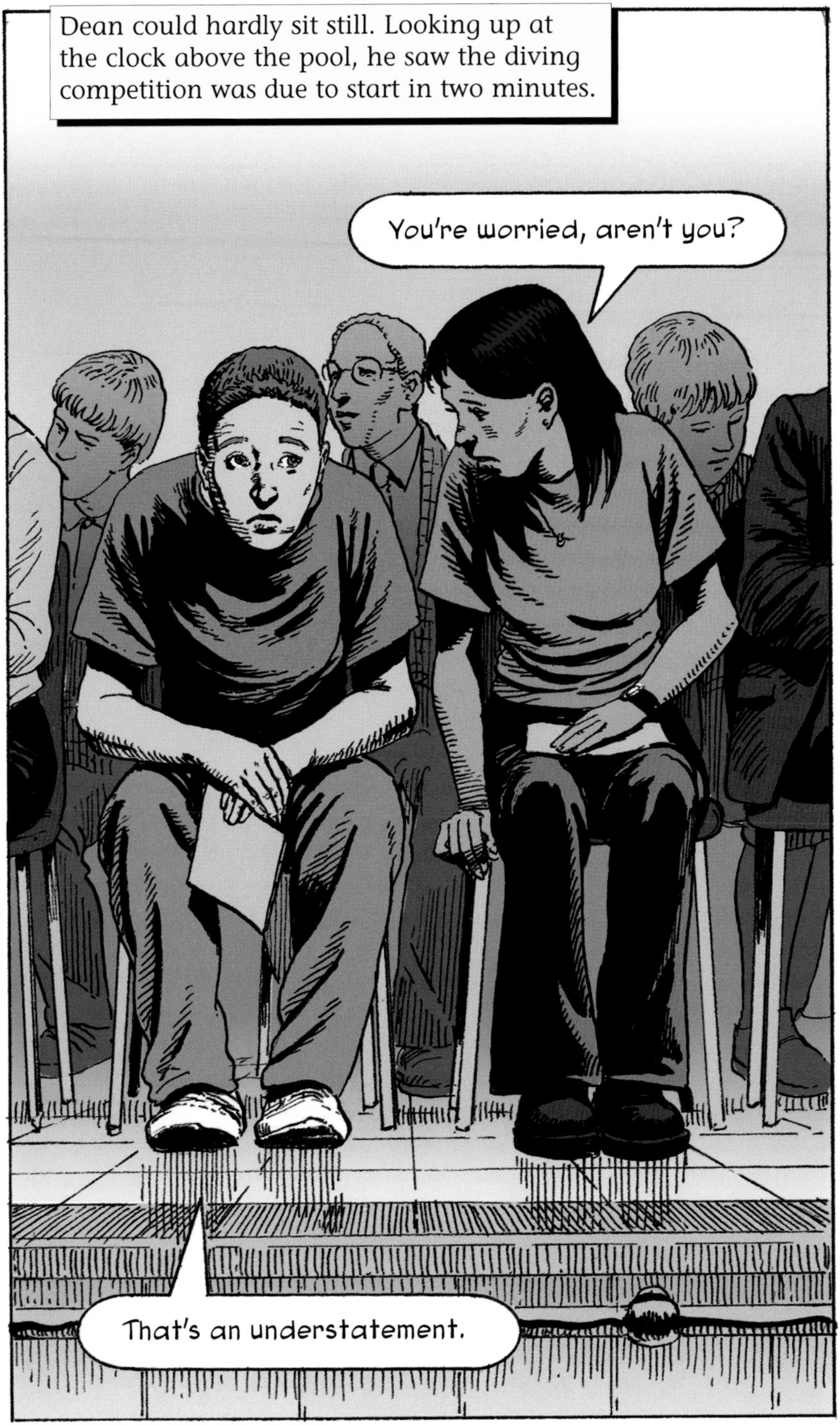
Dean could hardly sit still. Looking up at the clock above the pool, he saw the diving competition was due to start in two minutes.
You're worried, aren't you?
That's an understatement.

Dean was out of his mind with worry. He could see his brother would be the first to dive.

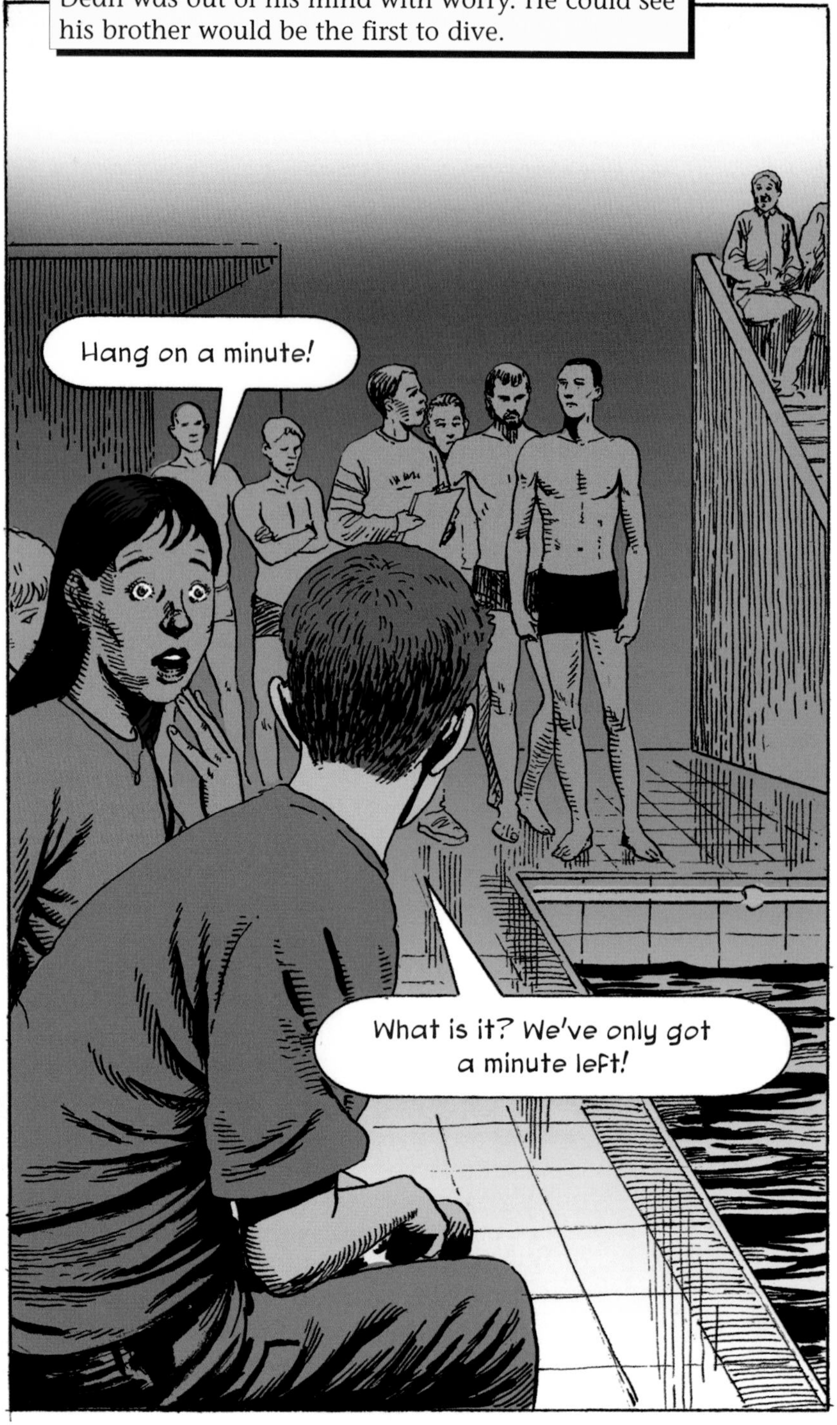
Hang on a minute!
What is it? We've only got a minute left!

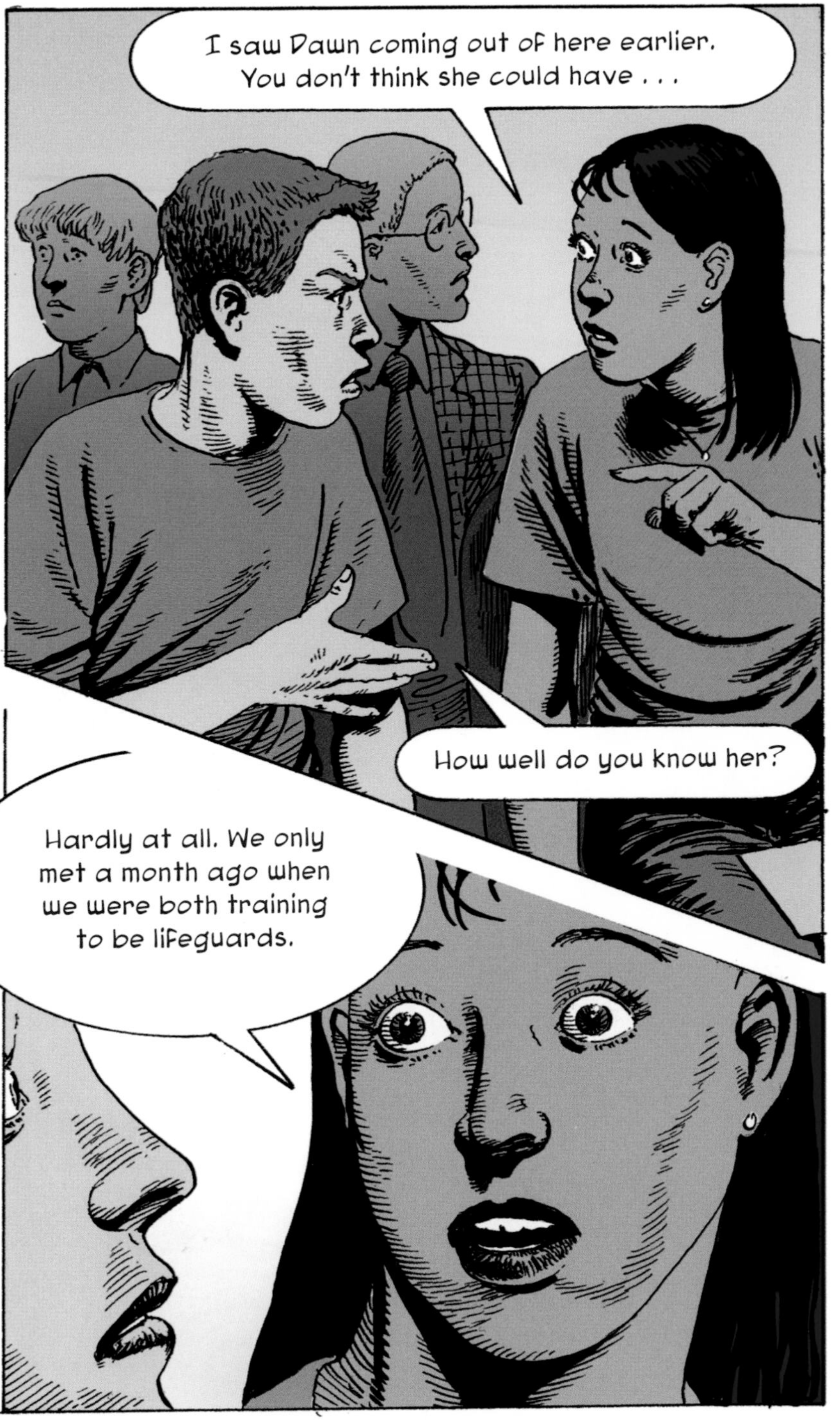
I saw Dawn coming out of here earlier. You don't think she could have . . .
How well do you know her?
Hardly at all. We only met a month ago when we were both training to be lifeguards.

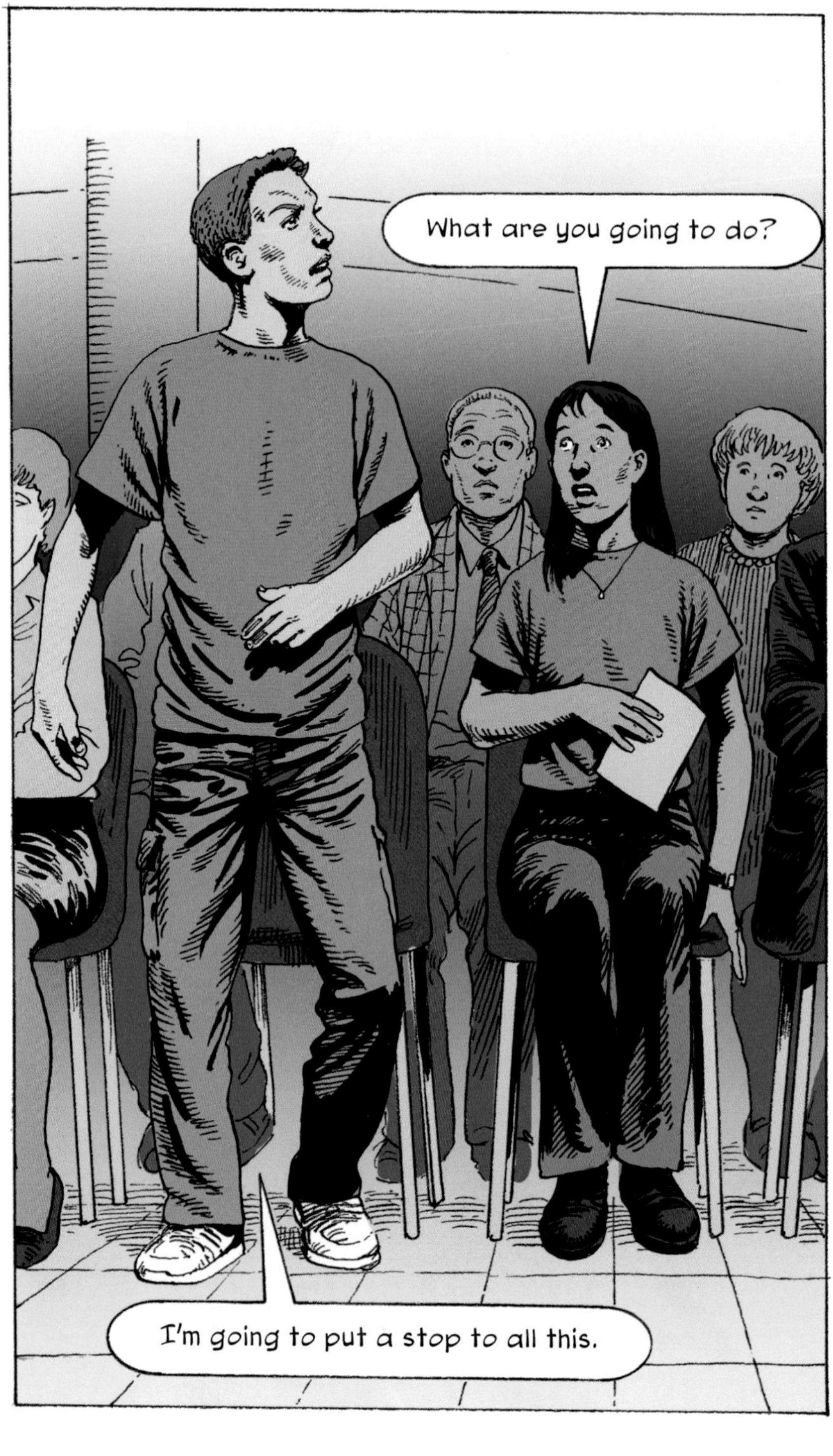
What are you going to do?
I'm going to put a stop to all this.

Ken Drake rose to his feet and grabbed the microphone.

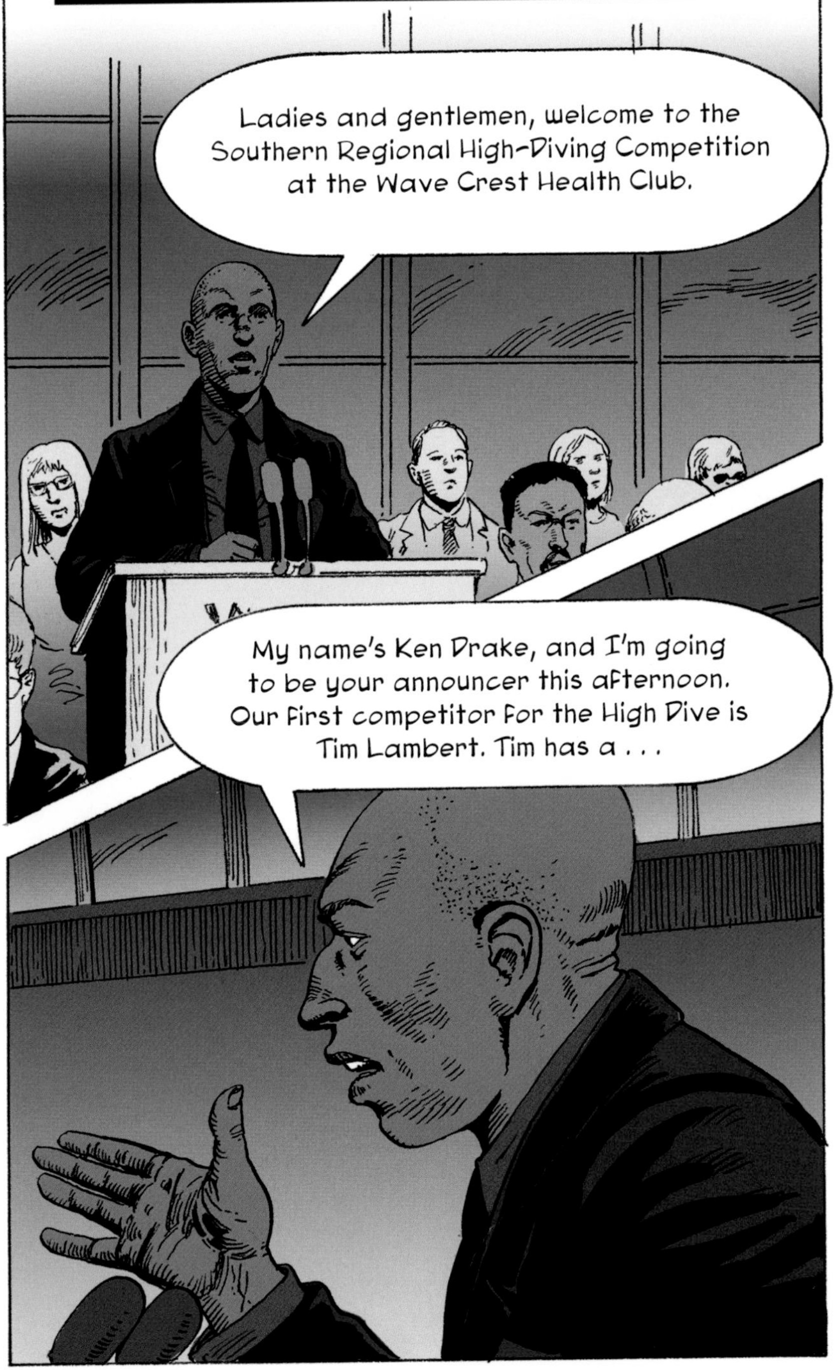
Ladies and gentlemen, welcome to the Southern Regional High-Diving Competition at the Wave Crest Health Club.
My name's Ken Drake, and I'm going to be your announcer this afternoon. Our first competitor for the High Dive is Tim Lambert. Tim has a . . .

Dean was no longer listening.

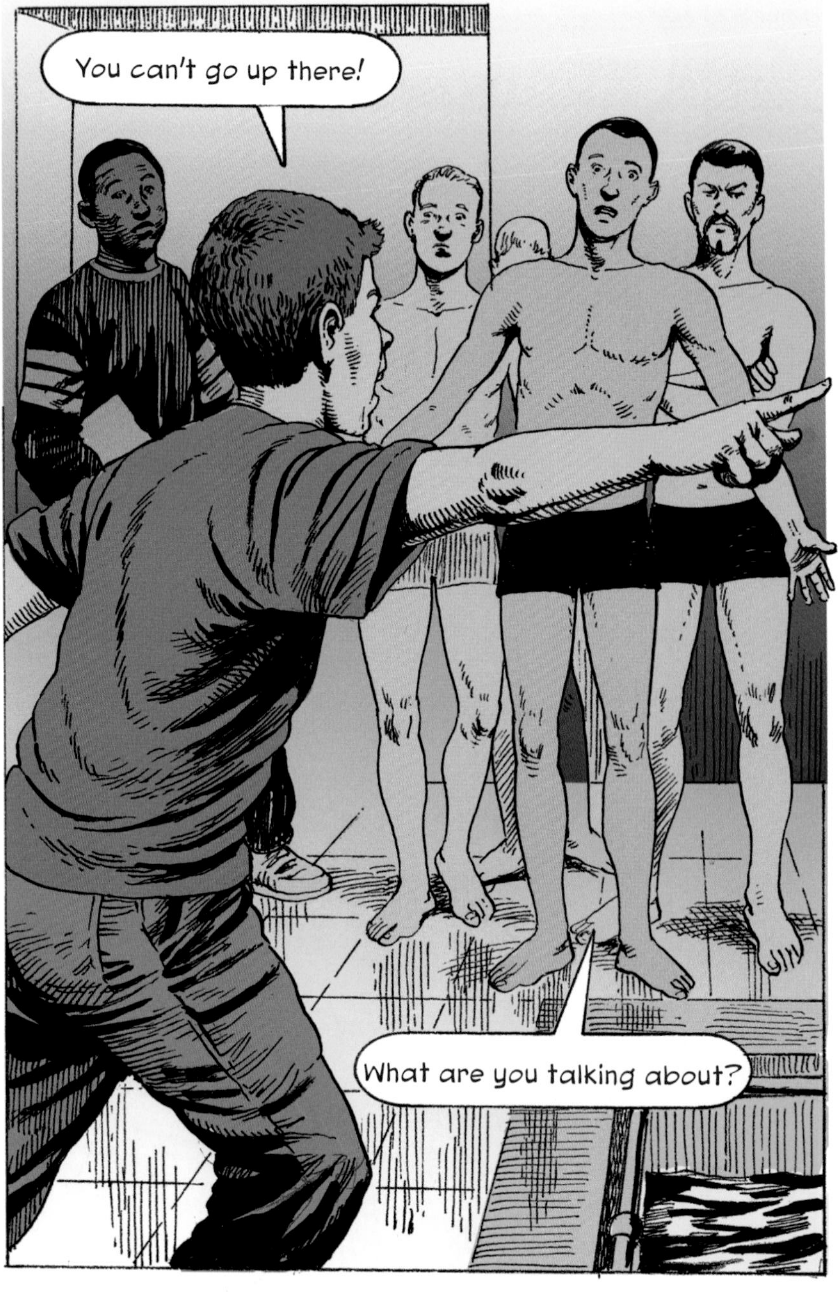

You can't go up there!
What are you talking about?

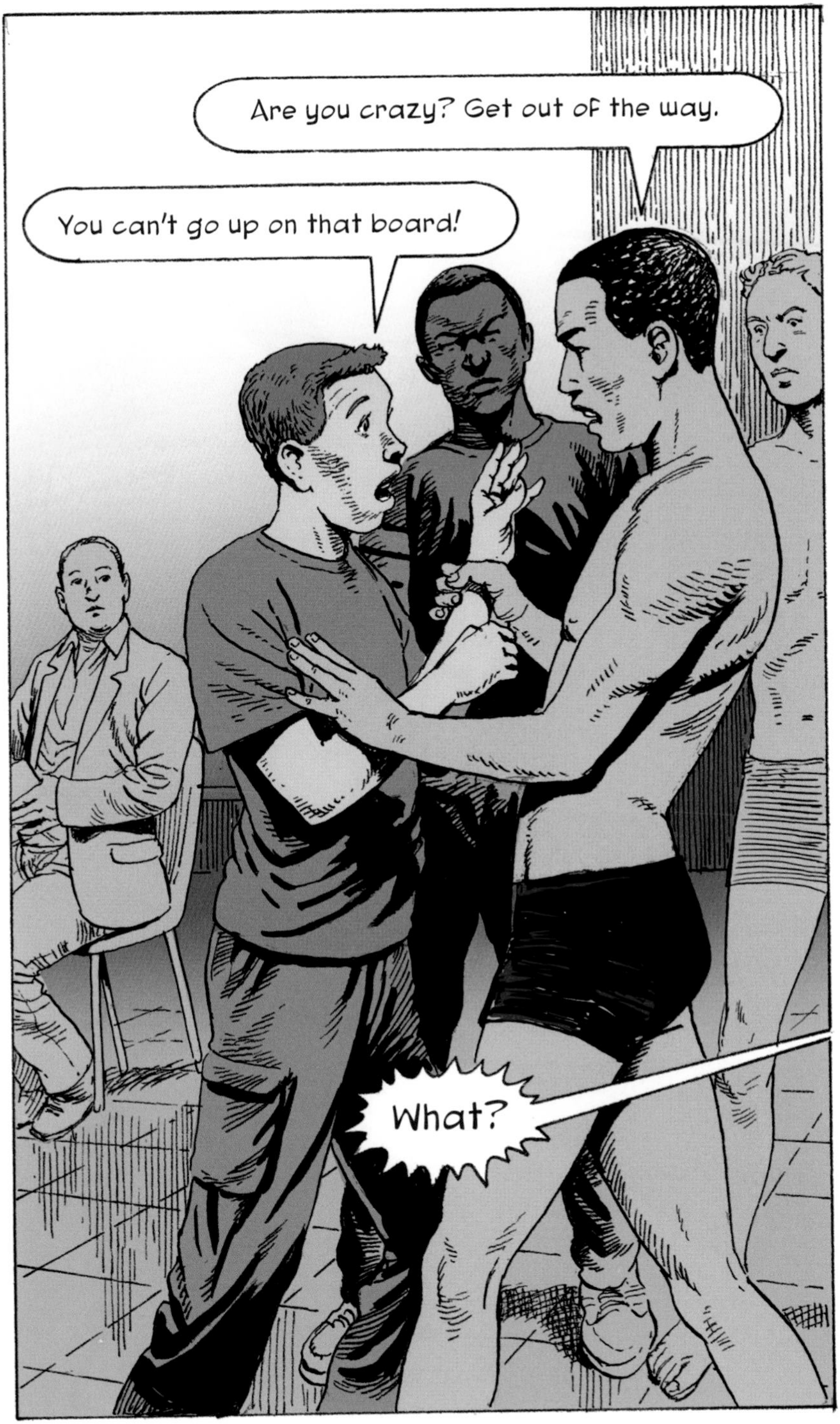
You can't go up on that board!
Are you crazy? Get out of the way.
What?

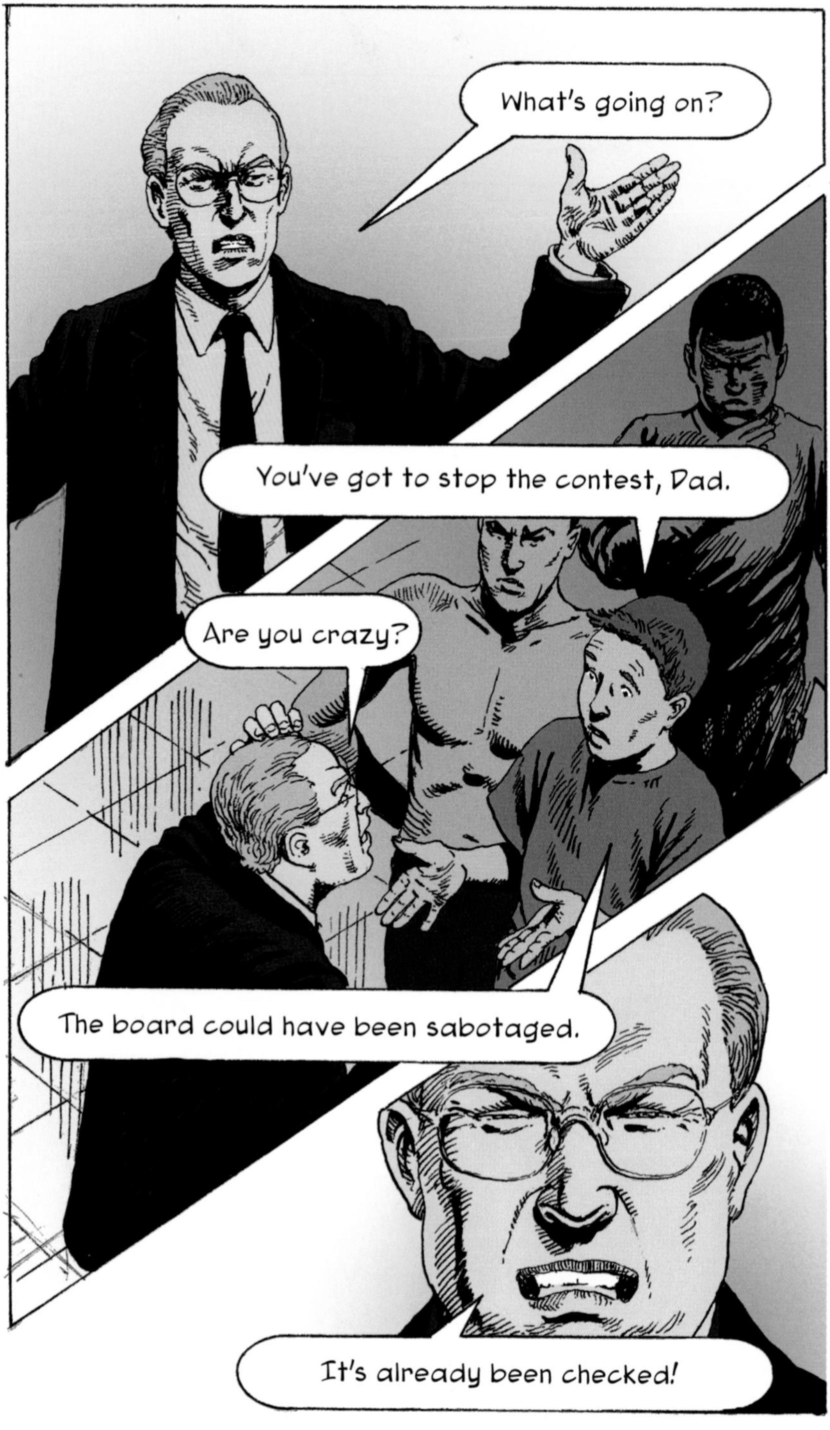
What's going on?
You've got to stop the contest, Dad.
Are you crazy?
The board could have been sabotaged.
It's already been checked!

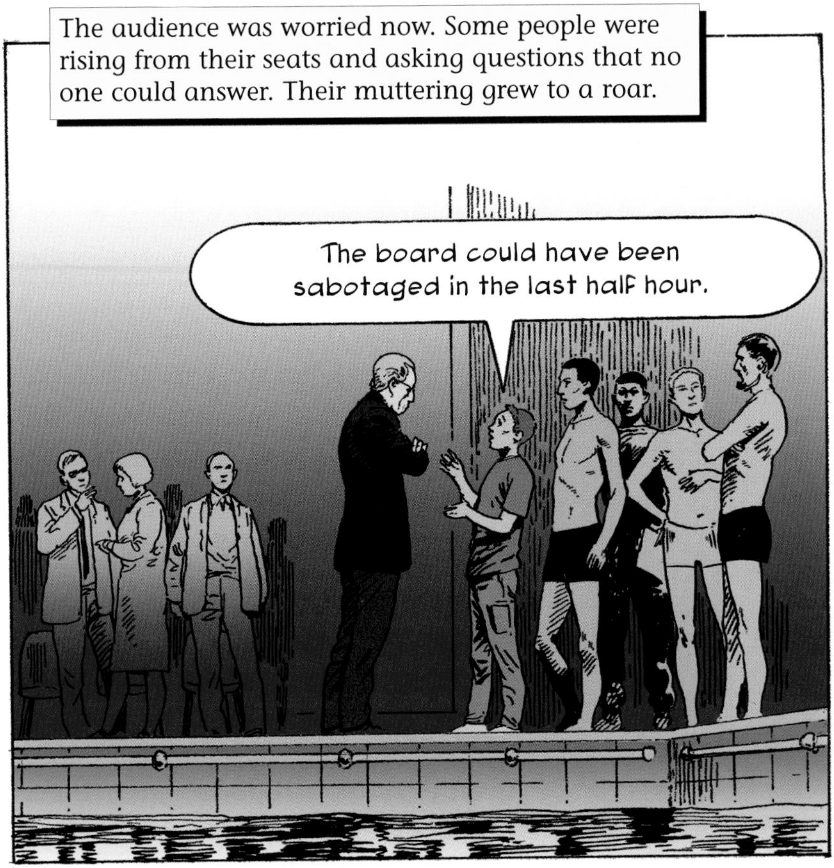
The audience was worried now. Some people were rising from their seats and asking questions that no one could answer. Their muttering grew to a roar.
The board could have been sabotaged in the last half hour.

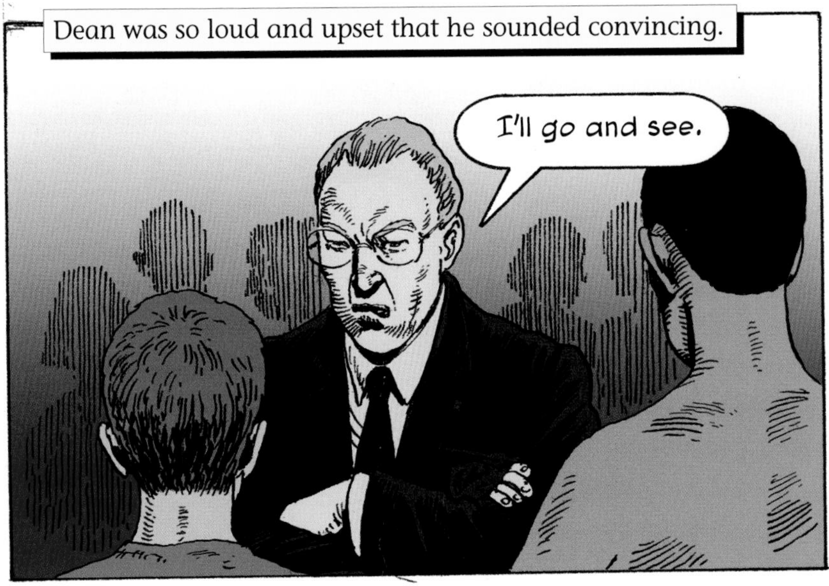
Dean was so loud and upset that he sounded convincing.
I'll go and see.

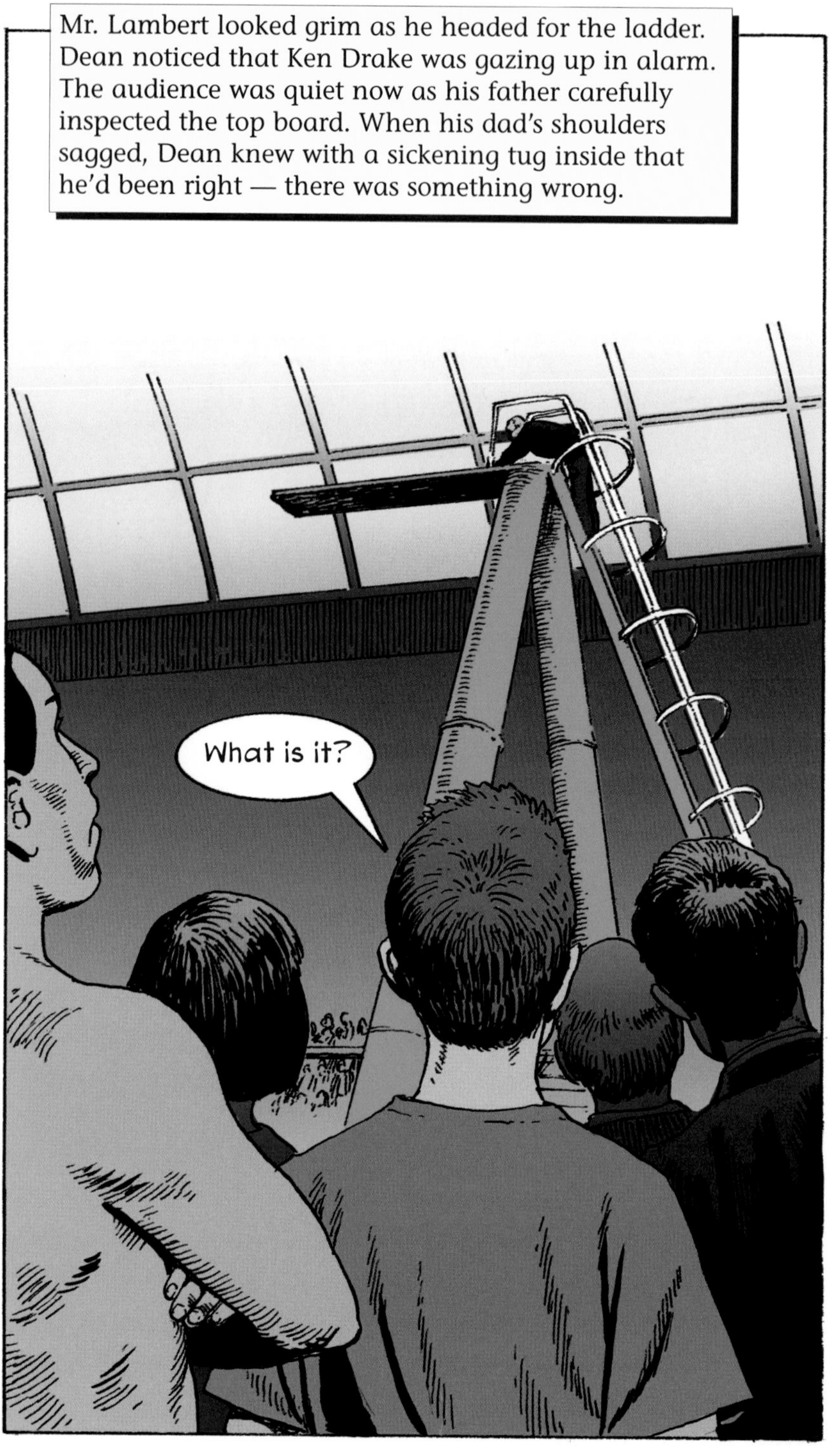
Mr. Lambert looked grim as he headed for the ladder. Dean noticed that Ken Drake was gazing up in alarm. The audience was quiet now as his father carefully inspected the top board. When his dad's shoulders sagged, Dean knew with a sickening tug inside that he'd been right — there was something wrong.
What is it?

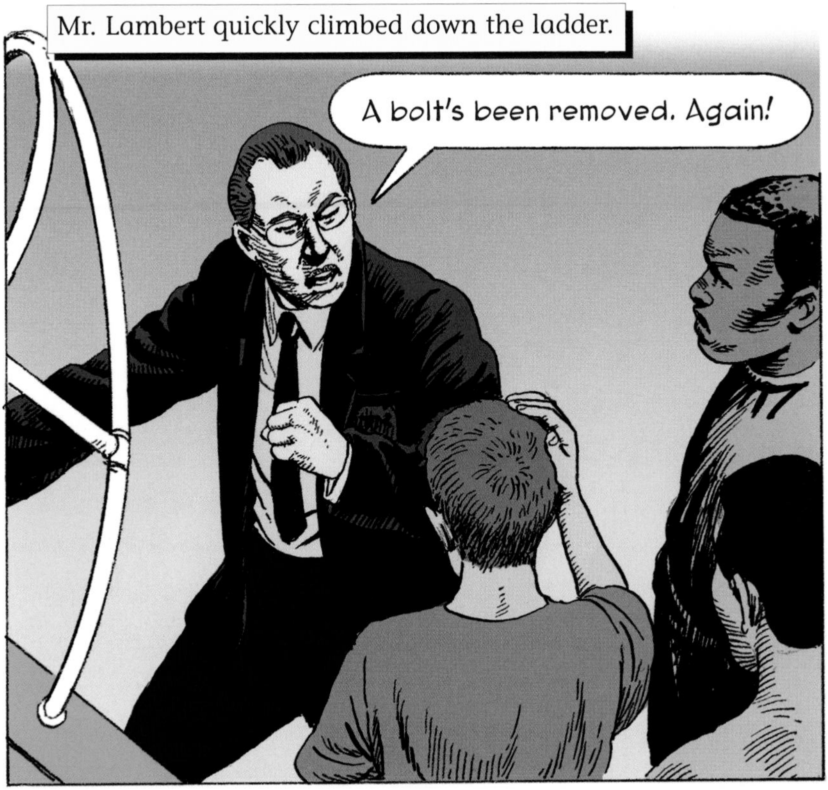
Mr. Lambert quickly climbed down the ladder.
A bolt's been removed. Again!

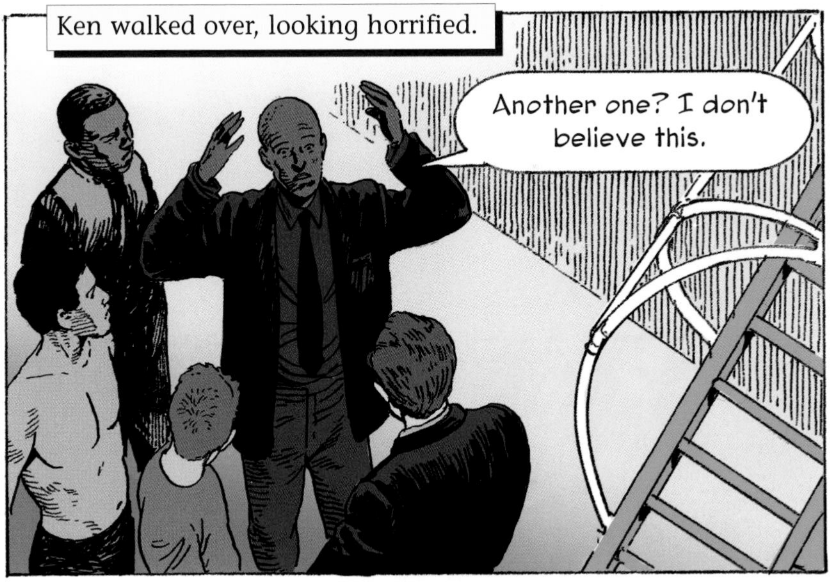
Ken walked over, looking horrified.
Another one? I don't believe this.

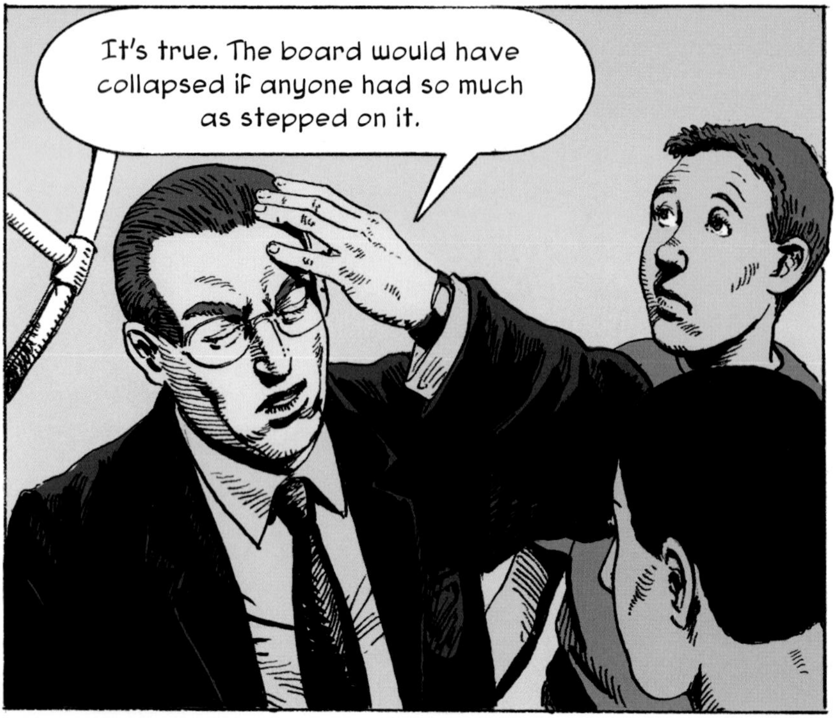
It's true. The board would have collapsed if anyone had so much as stepped on it.

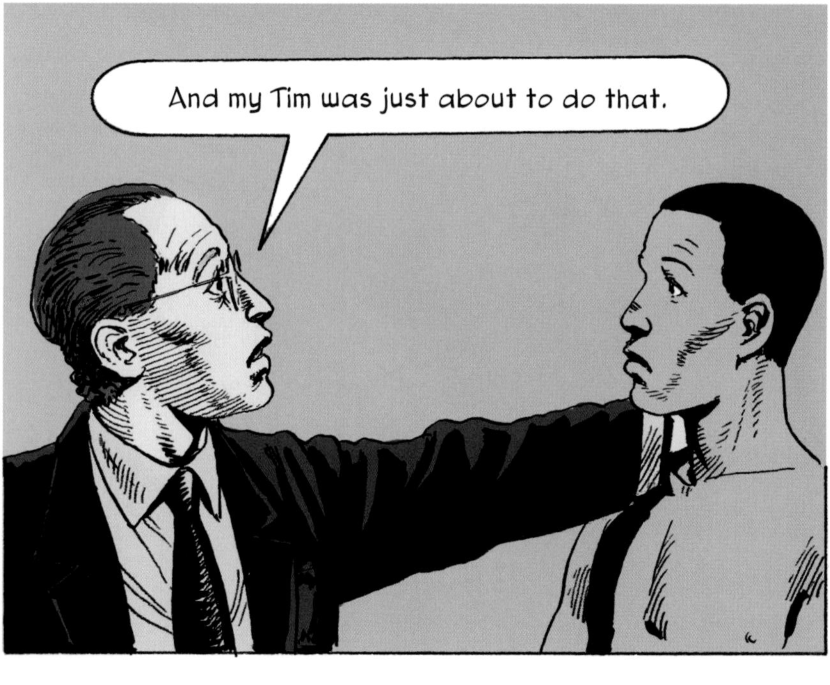
And my Tim was just about to do that.

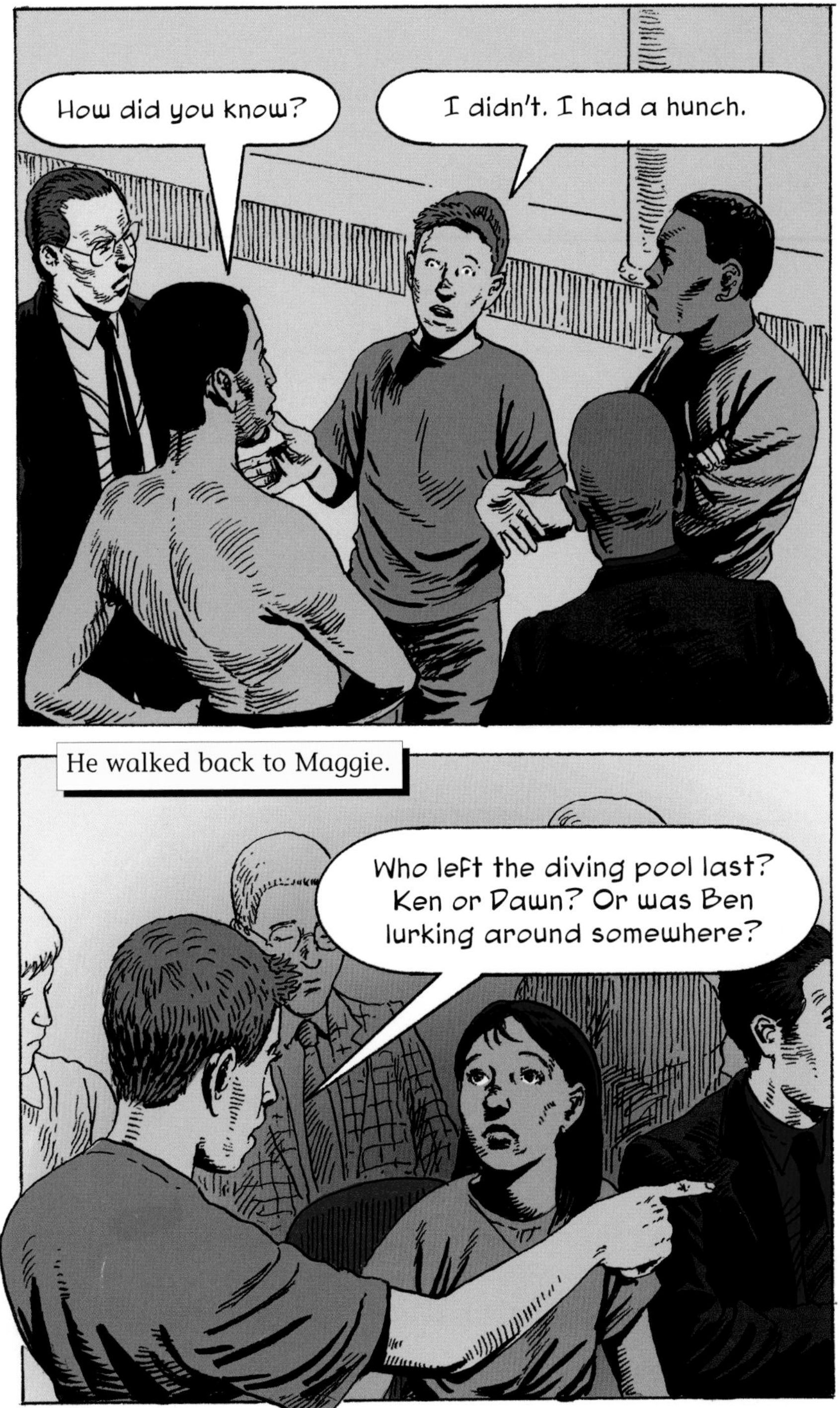
How did you know?
I didn't. I had a hunch.
He walked back to Maggie.
Who left the diving pool last? Ken or Dawn? Or was Ben lurking around somewhere?

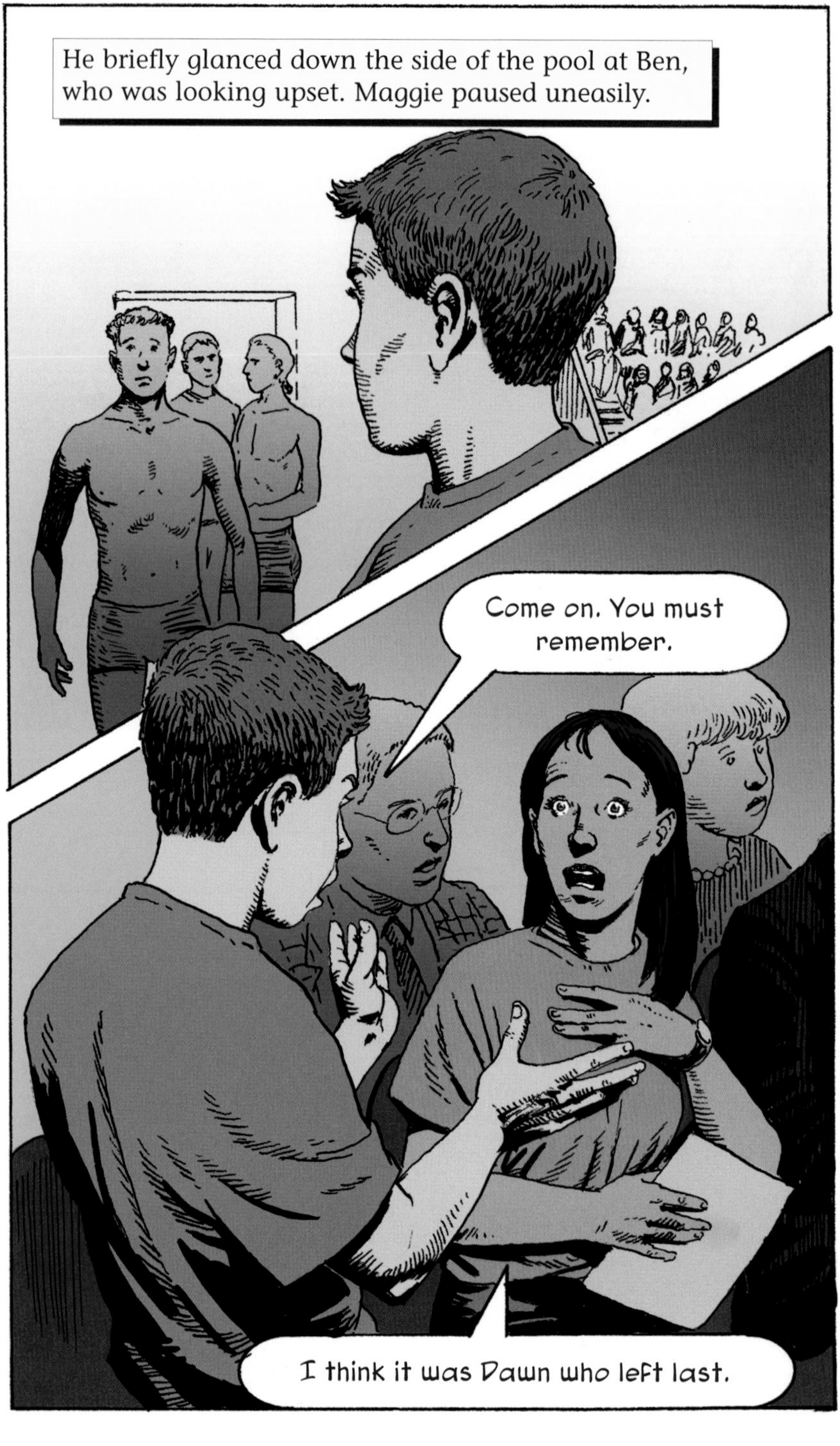
He briefly glanced down the side of the pool at Ben, who was looking upset. Maggie paused uneasily.
Come on. You must remember.
I think it was Dawn who left last.

CHAPTER SIX

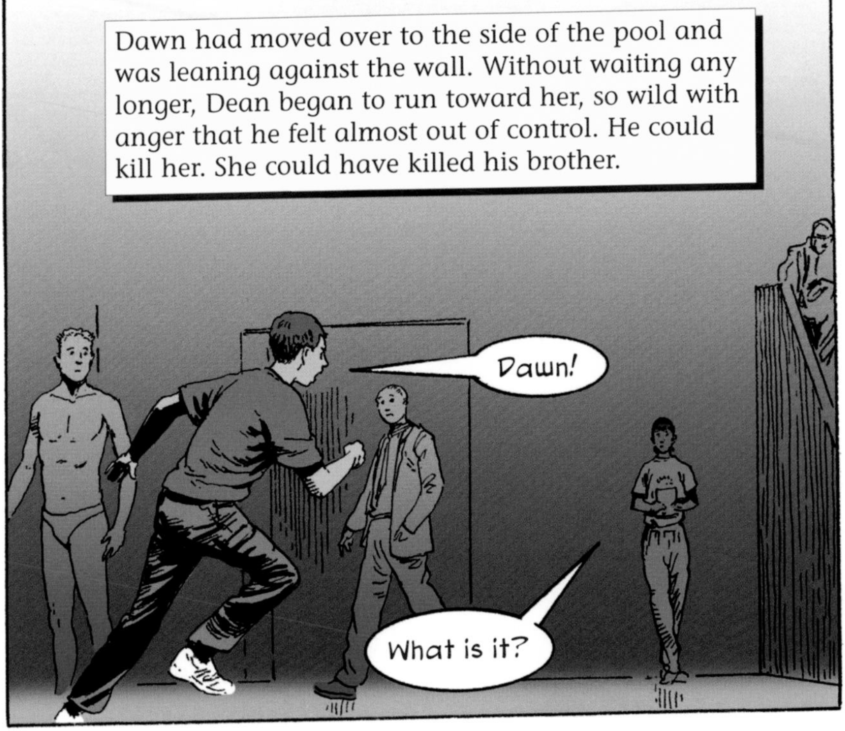
Dawn had moved over to the side of the pool and was leaning against the wall. Without waiting any longer, Dean began to run toward her, so wild with anger that he felt almost out of control. He could kill her. She could have killed his brother.
Dawn!
What is it?

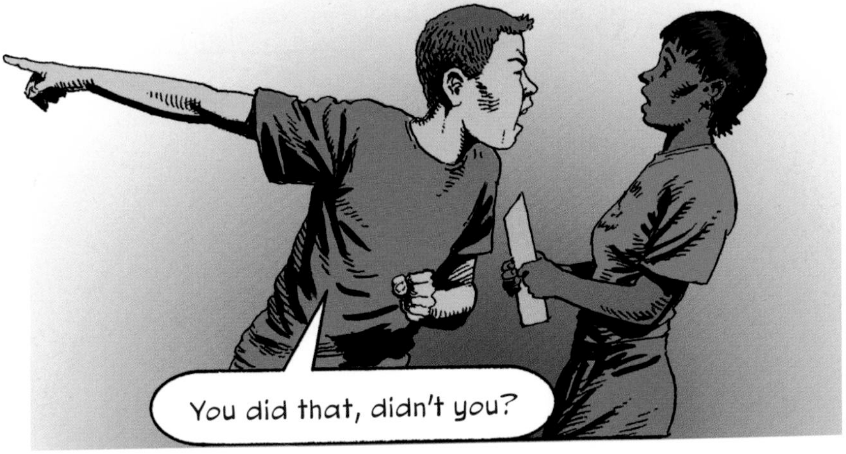
You did that, didn't you?

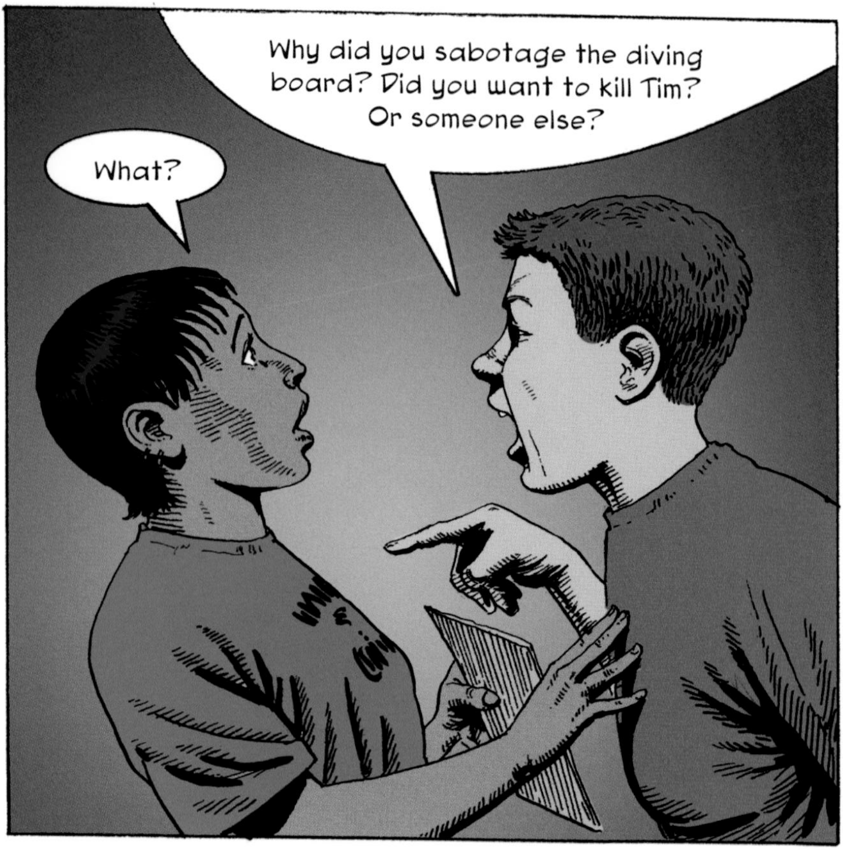
Why did you sabotage the diving board? Did you want to kill Tim? Or someone else?
What?

Dawn looked at him in shock.

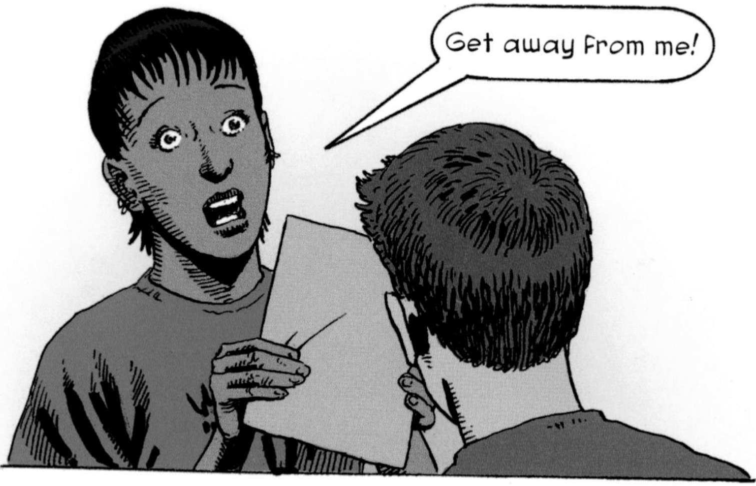
Get away from me!

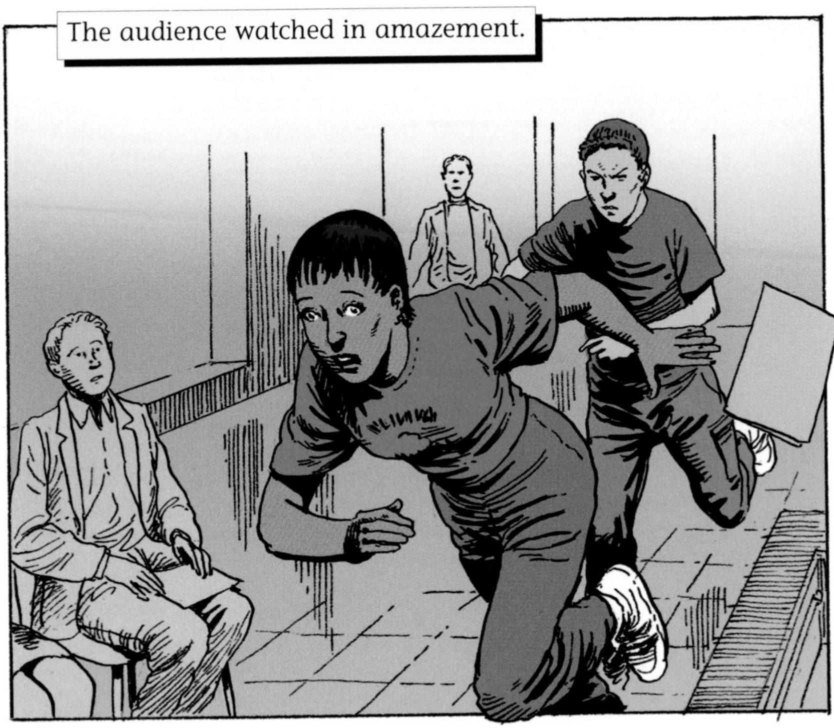
The audience watched in amazement.

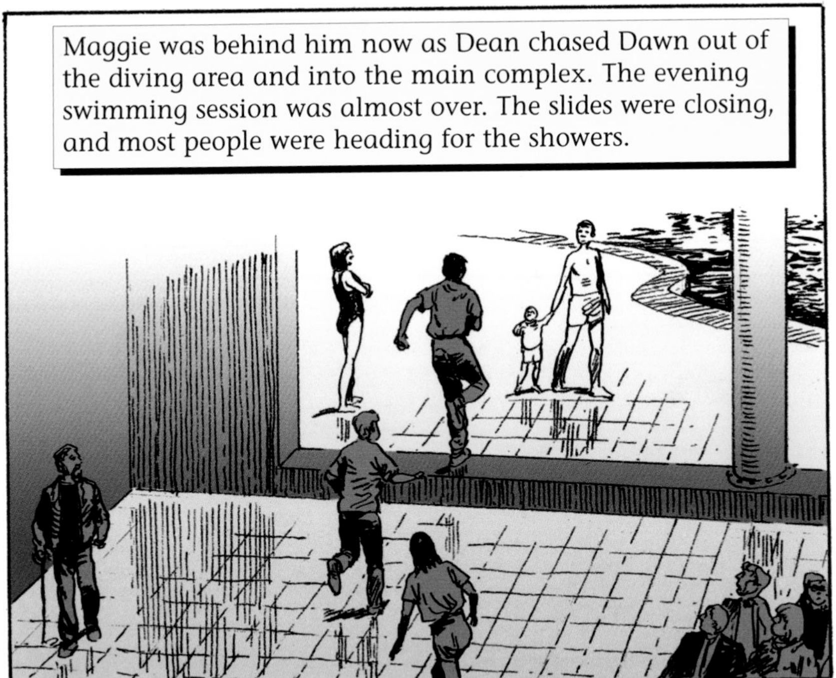
Maggie was behind him now as Dean chased Dawn out of the diving area and into the main complex. The evening swimming session was almost over. The slides were closing, and most people were heading for the showers.

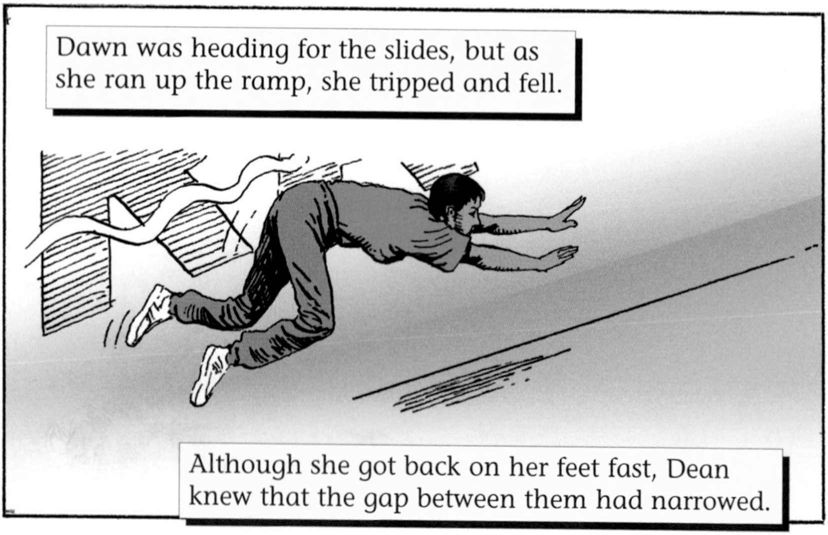
Dawn was heading for the slides, but as she ran up the ramp, she tripped and fell.
Although she got back on her feet fast, Dean knew that the gap between them had narrowed.

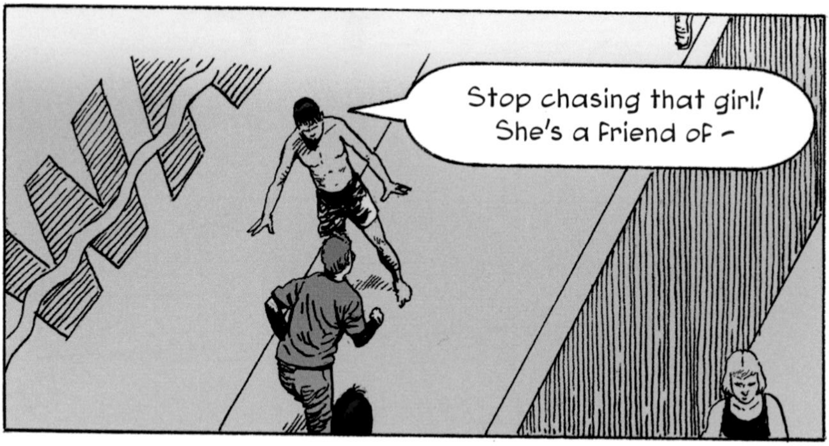
Stop chasing that girl! She's a friend of -

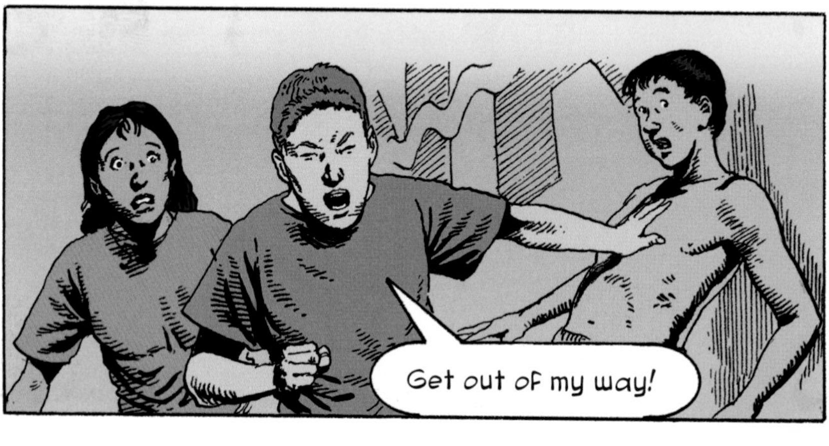
Get out of my way!

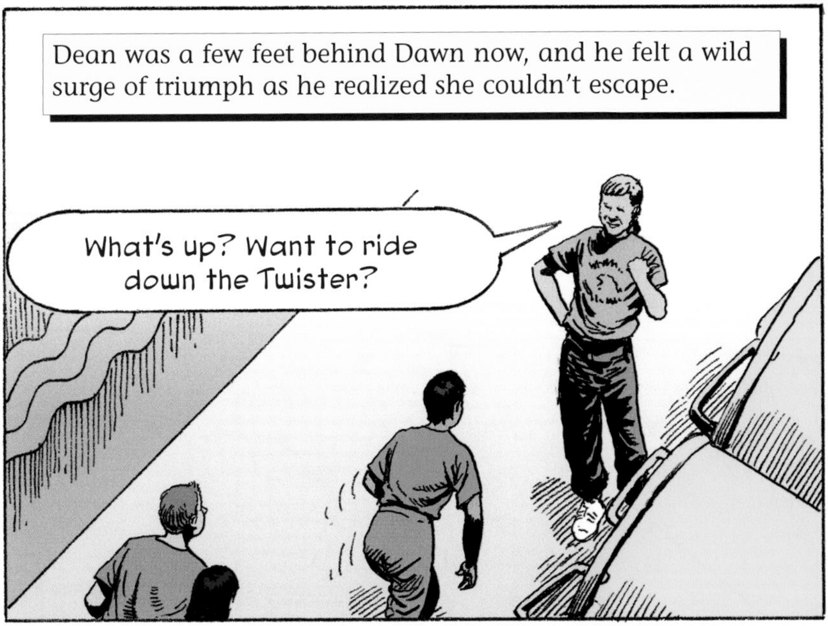
Dean was a few feet behind Dawn now, and he felt a wild surge of triumph as he realized she couldn't escape.
What's up? Want to ride down the Twister?

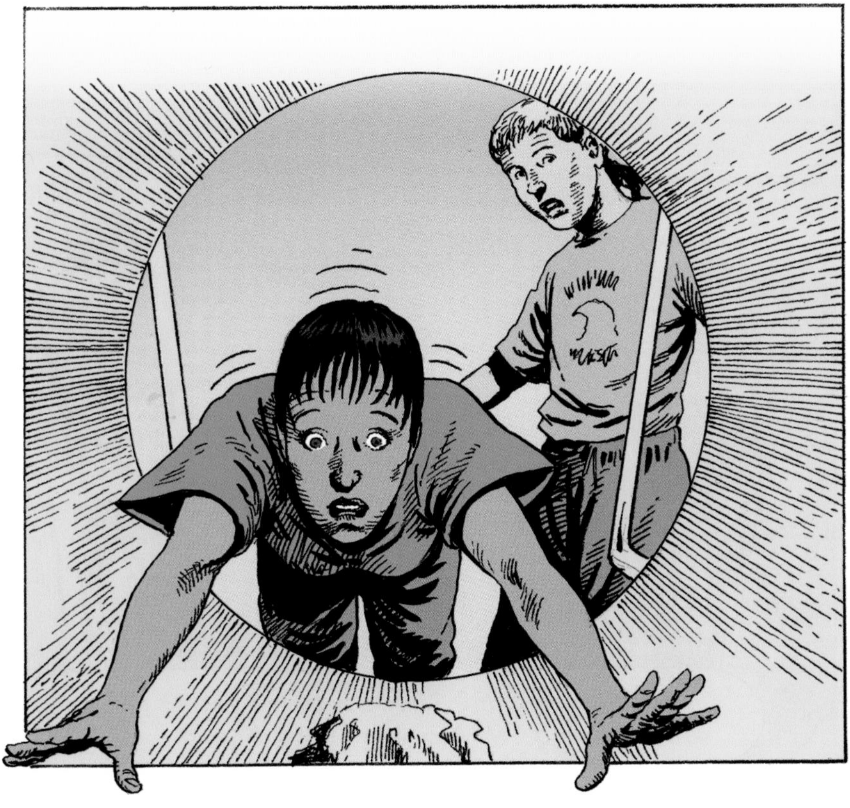

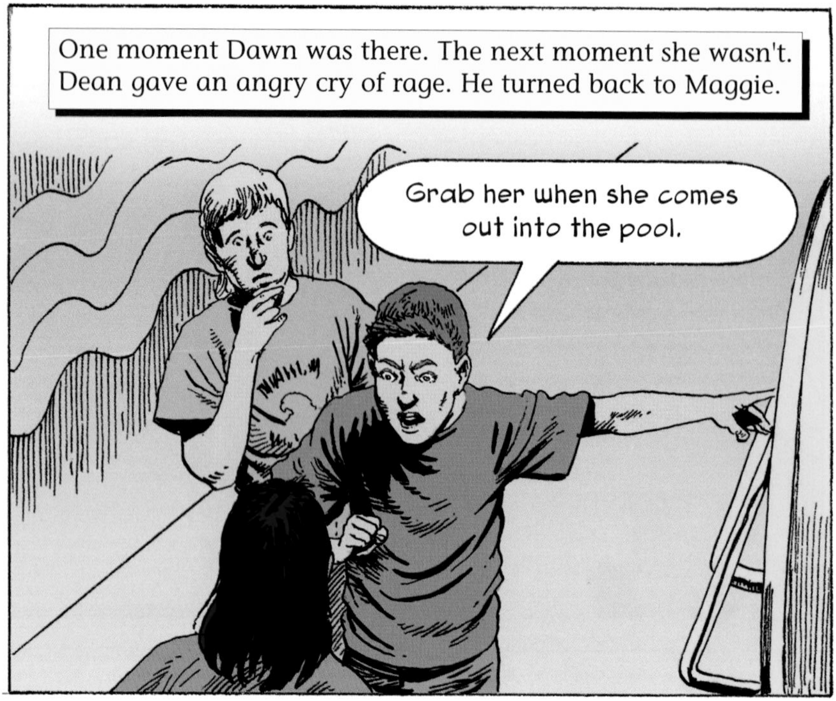
One moment Dawn was there. The next moment she wasn't. Dean gave an angry cry of rage. He turned back to Maggie.
Grab her when she comes out into the pool.

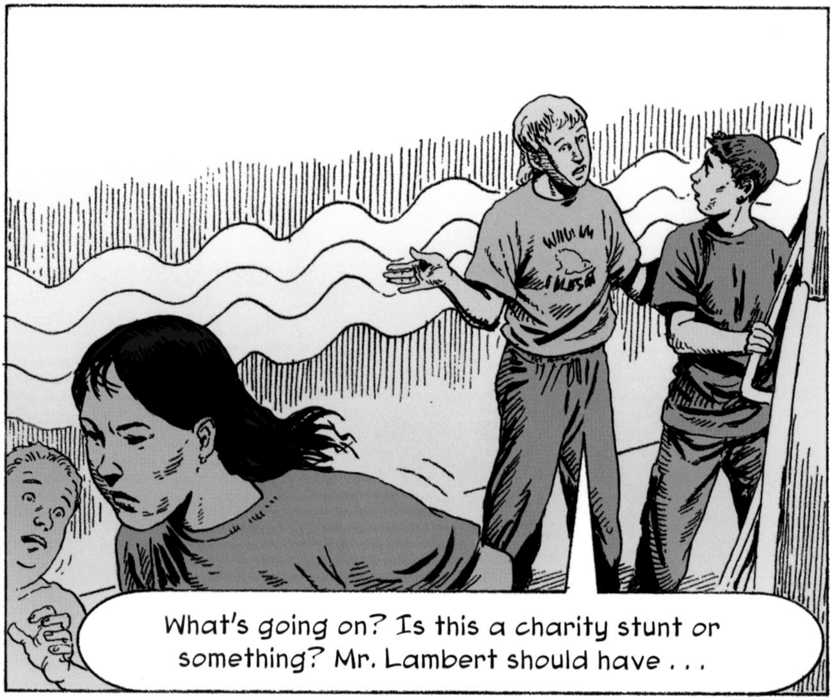
What's going on? Is this a charity stunt or something? Mr. Lambert should have . . .

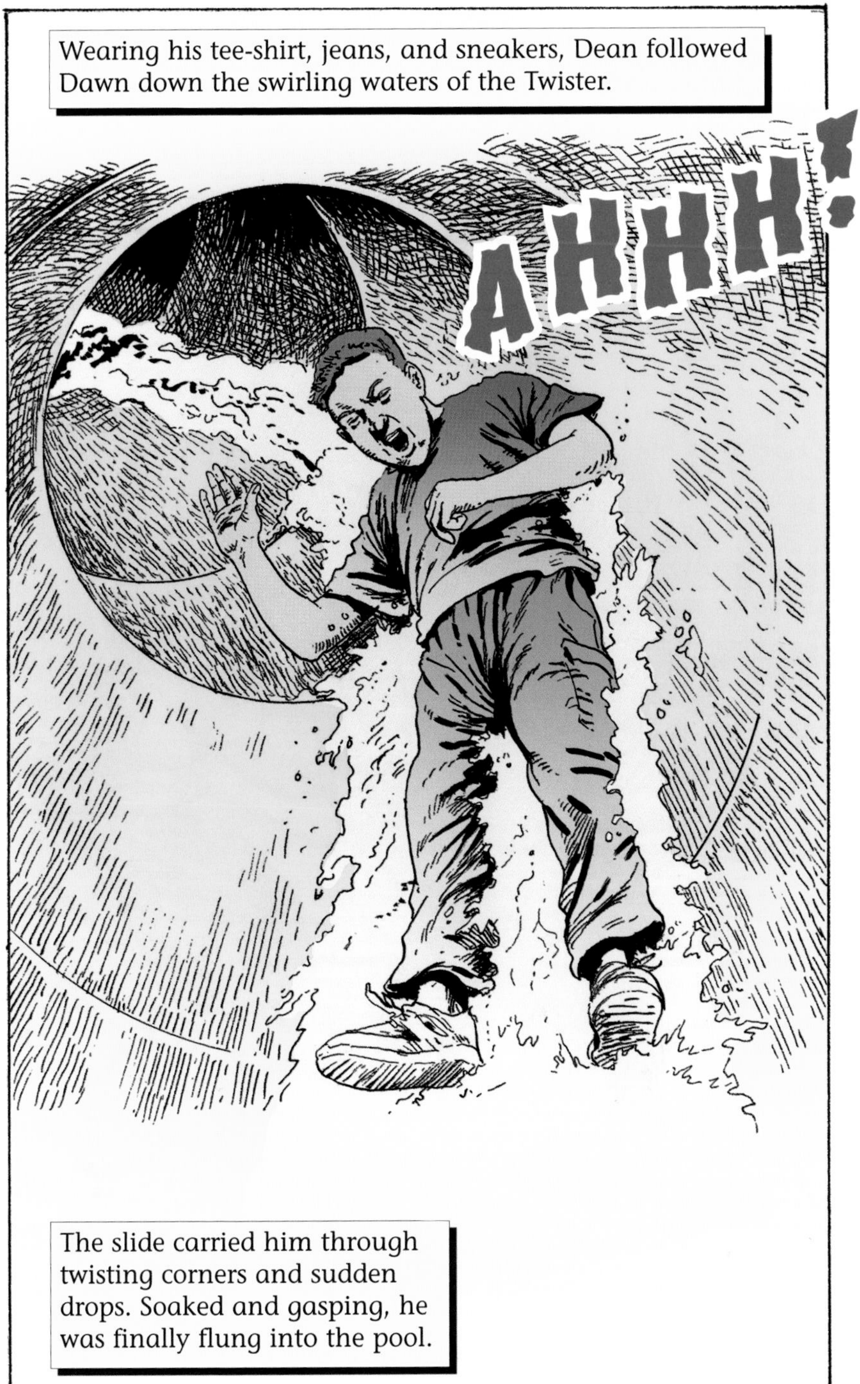
Wearing his tee-shirt, jeans, and sneakers, Dean followed Dawn down the swirling waters of the Twister.
AHHH!
The slide carried him through twisting corners and sudden drops. Soaked and gasping, he was finally flung into the pool.

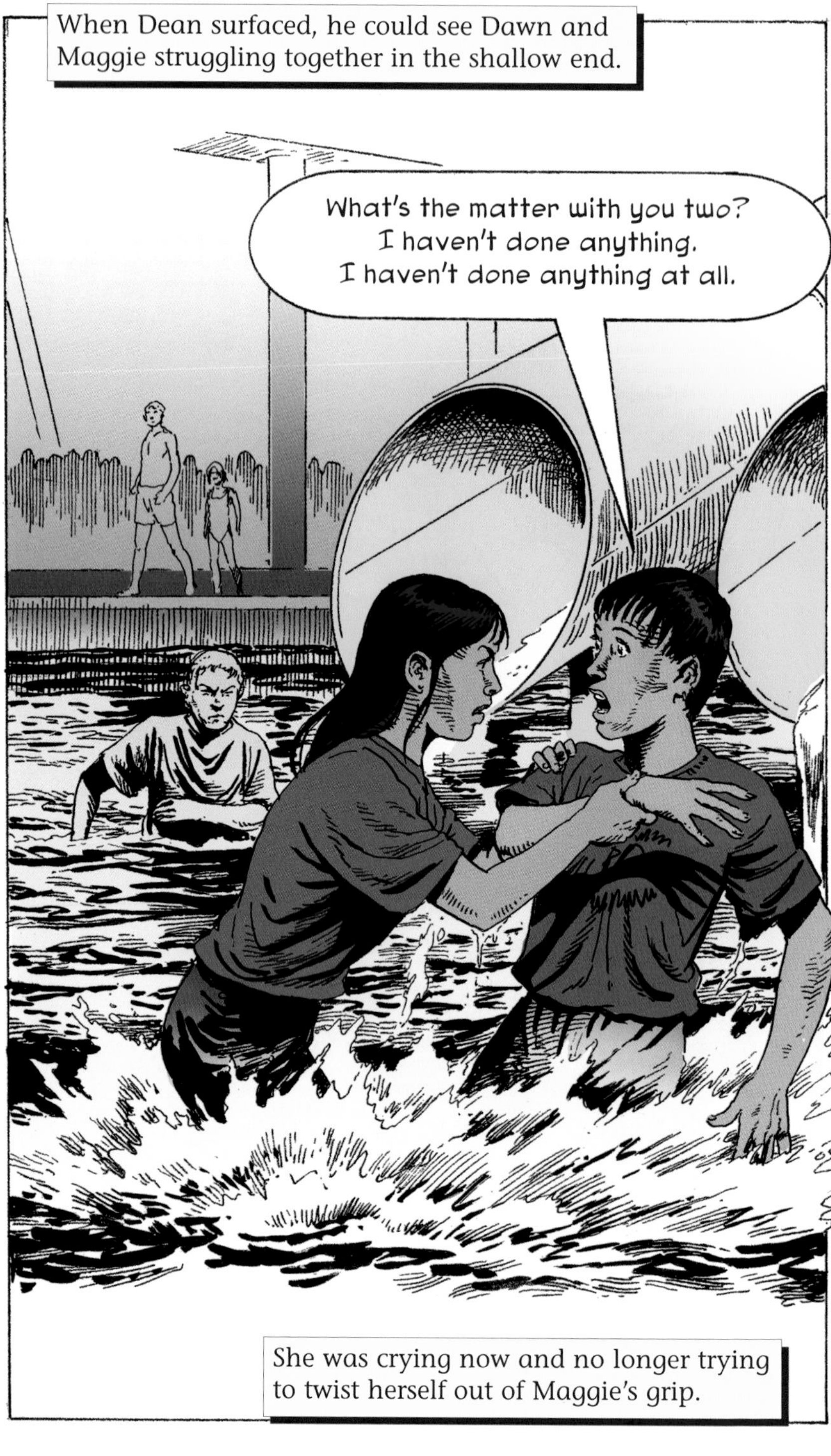
When Dean surfaced, he could see Dawn and Maggie struggling together in the shallow end.
What's the matter with you two? I haven't done anything. I haven't done anything at all.
She was crying now and no longer trying to twist herself out of Maggie's grip.

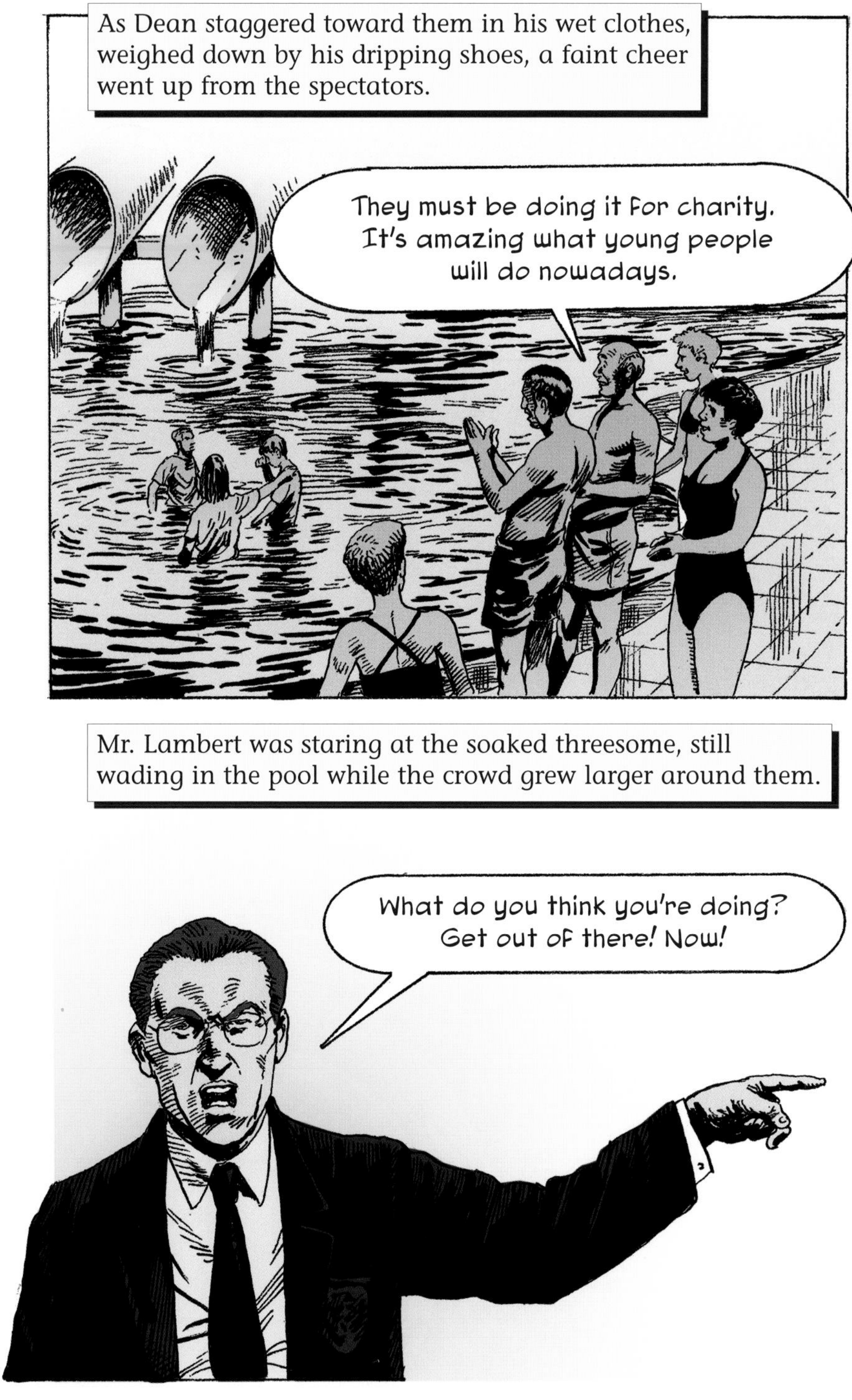
As Dean staggered toward them in his wet clothes, weighed down by his dripping shoes, a faint cheer went up from the spectators.
They must be doing it for charity. It's amazing what young people will do nowadays.
Mr. Lambert was staring at the soaked threesome, still wading in the pool while the crowd grew larger around them.
What do you think you're doing? Get out of there! Now!

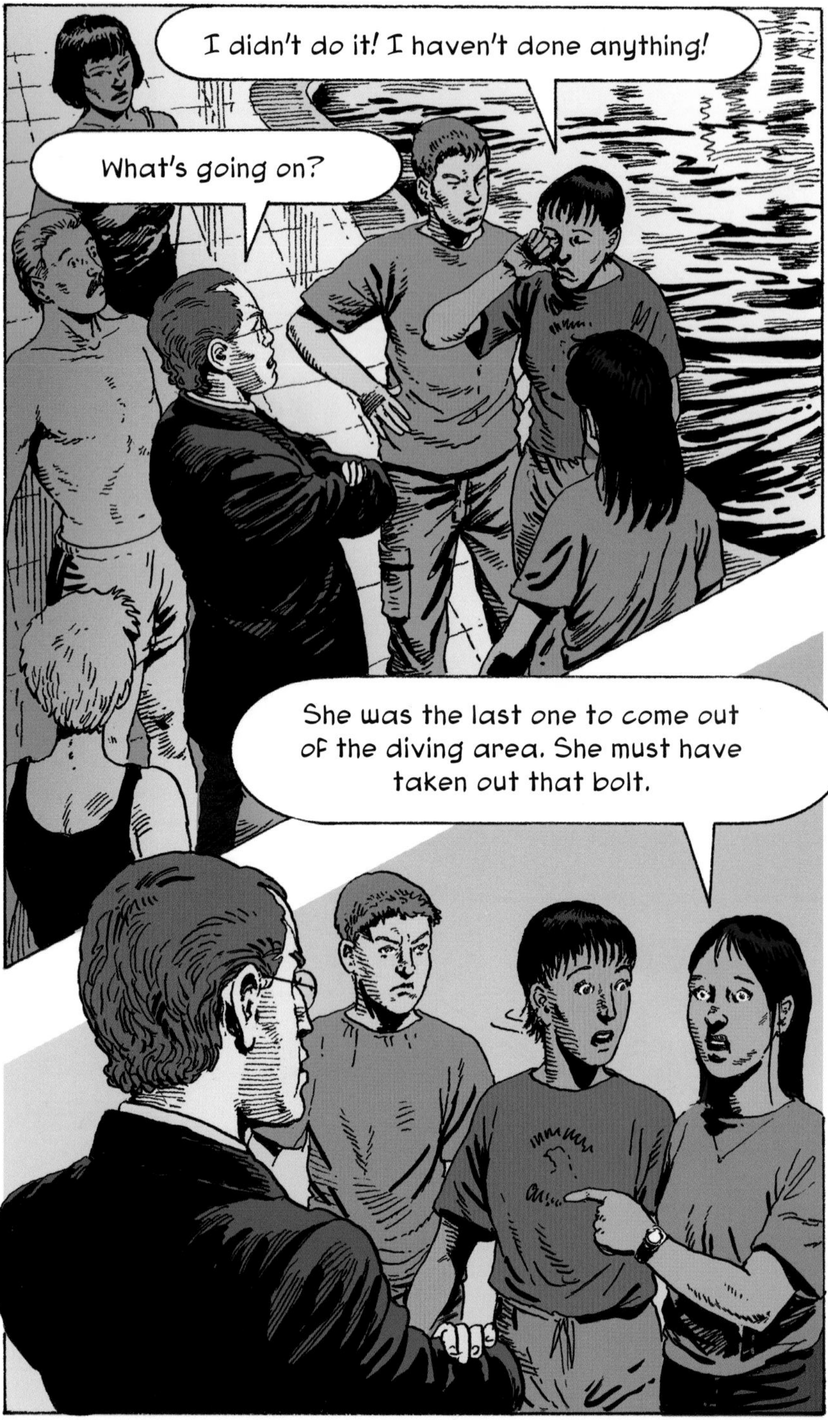
I didn't do it! I haven't done anything!
What's going on?
She was the last one to come out of the diving area. She must have taken out that bolt.

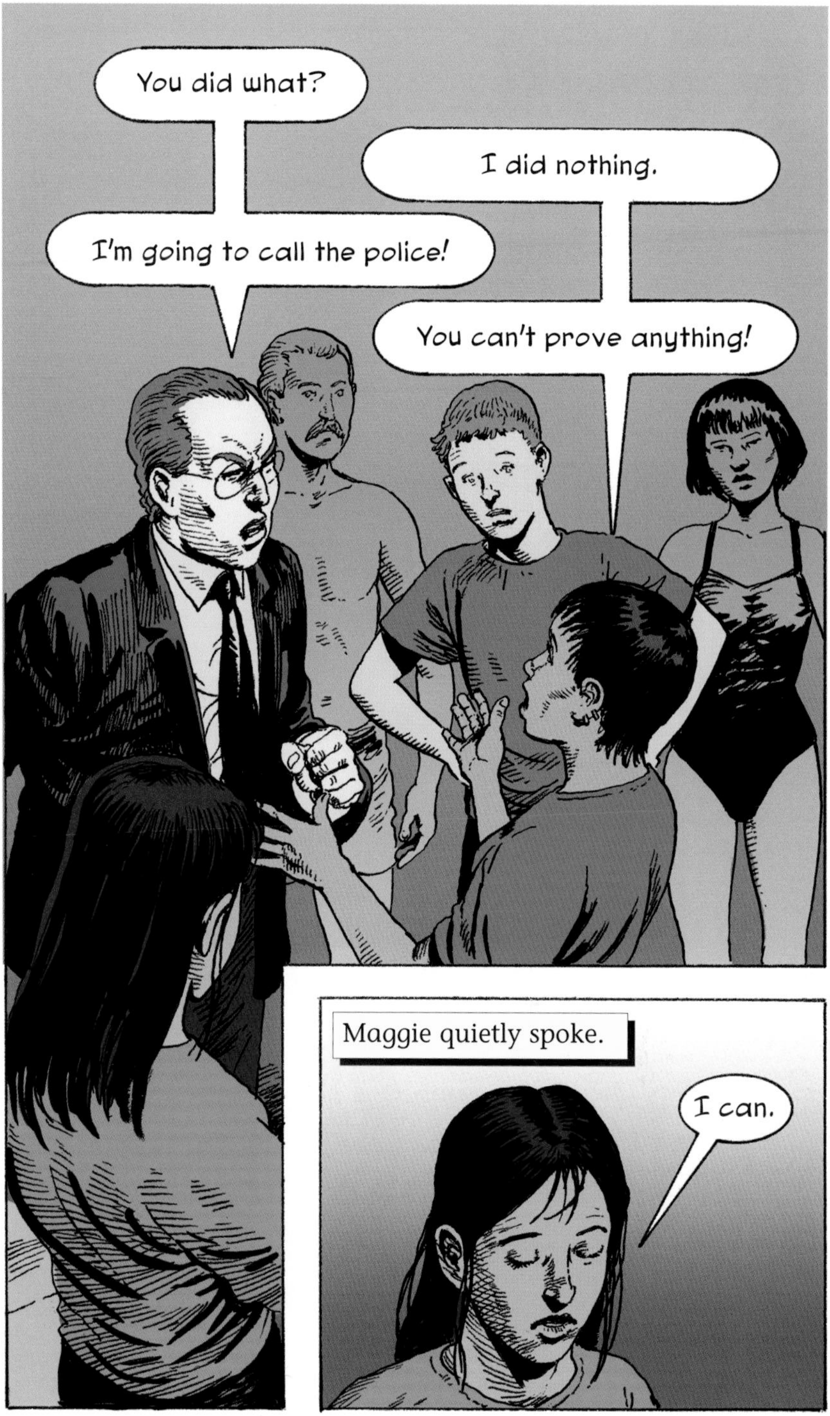
You did what?
I'm going to call the police!
I did nothing.
You can't prove anything!
Maggie quietly spoke.
I can.

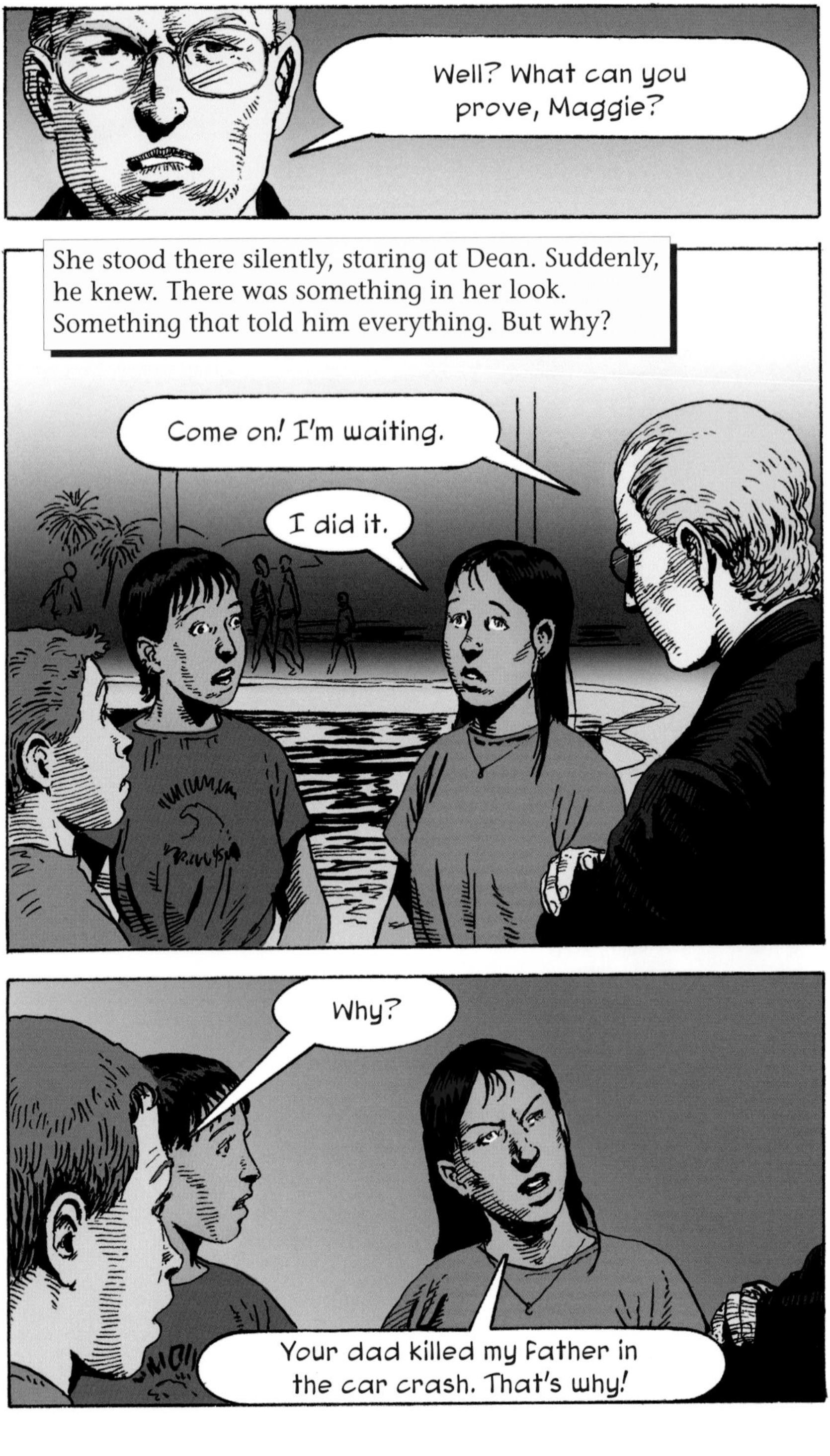
Well? What can you prove, Maggie?
She stood there silently, staring at Dean. Suddenly, he knew. There was something in her look. Something that told him everything. But why?
Come on! I'm waiting.
I did it.
Why?
Your dad killed my father in the car crash. That's why!

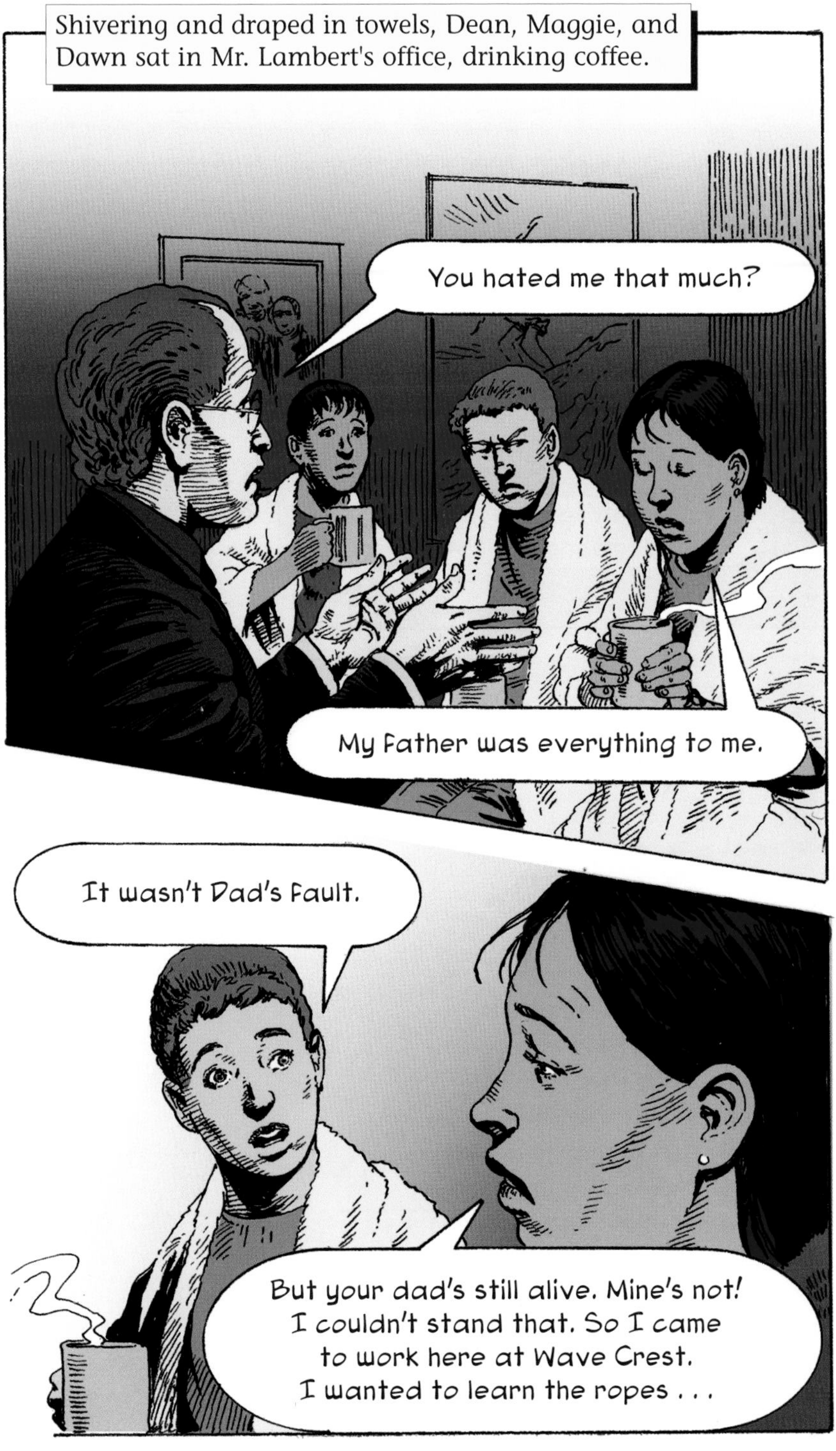
Shivering and draped in towels, Dean, Maggie, and Dawn sat in Mr. Lambert's office, drinking coffee.
You hated me that much?
My father was everything to me.
It wasn't Dad's fault.
But your dad's still alive. Mine's not! I couldn't stand that. So I came to work here at Wave Crest. I wanted to learn the ropes . . .

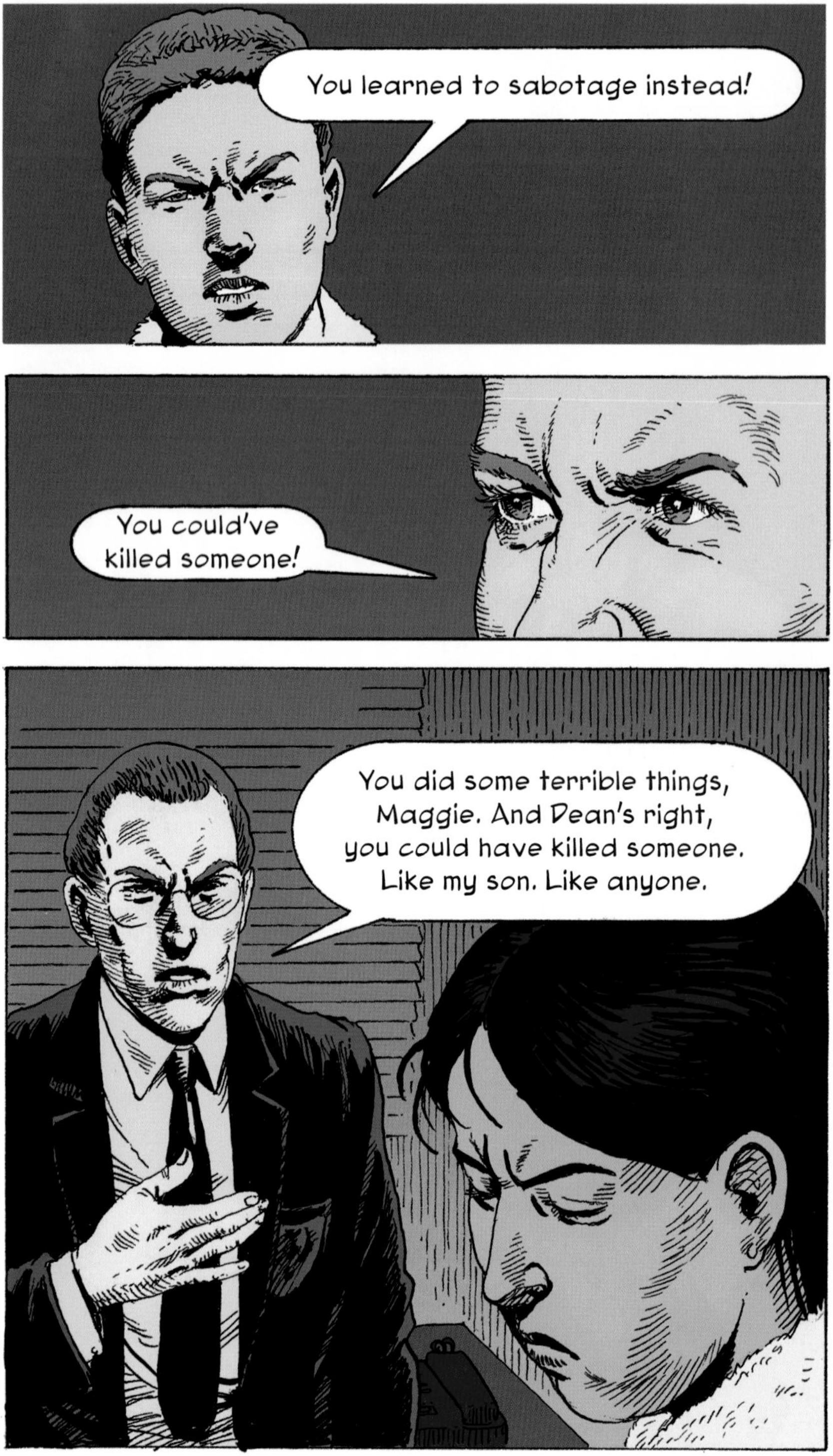
You learned to sabotage instead!
You could've killed someone!
You did some terrible things, Maggie. And Dean's right, you could have killed someone. Like my son. Like anyone.

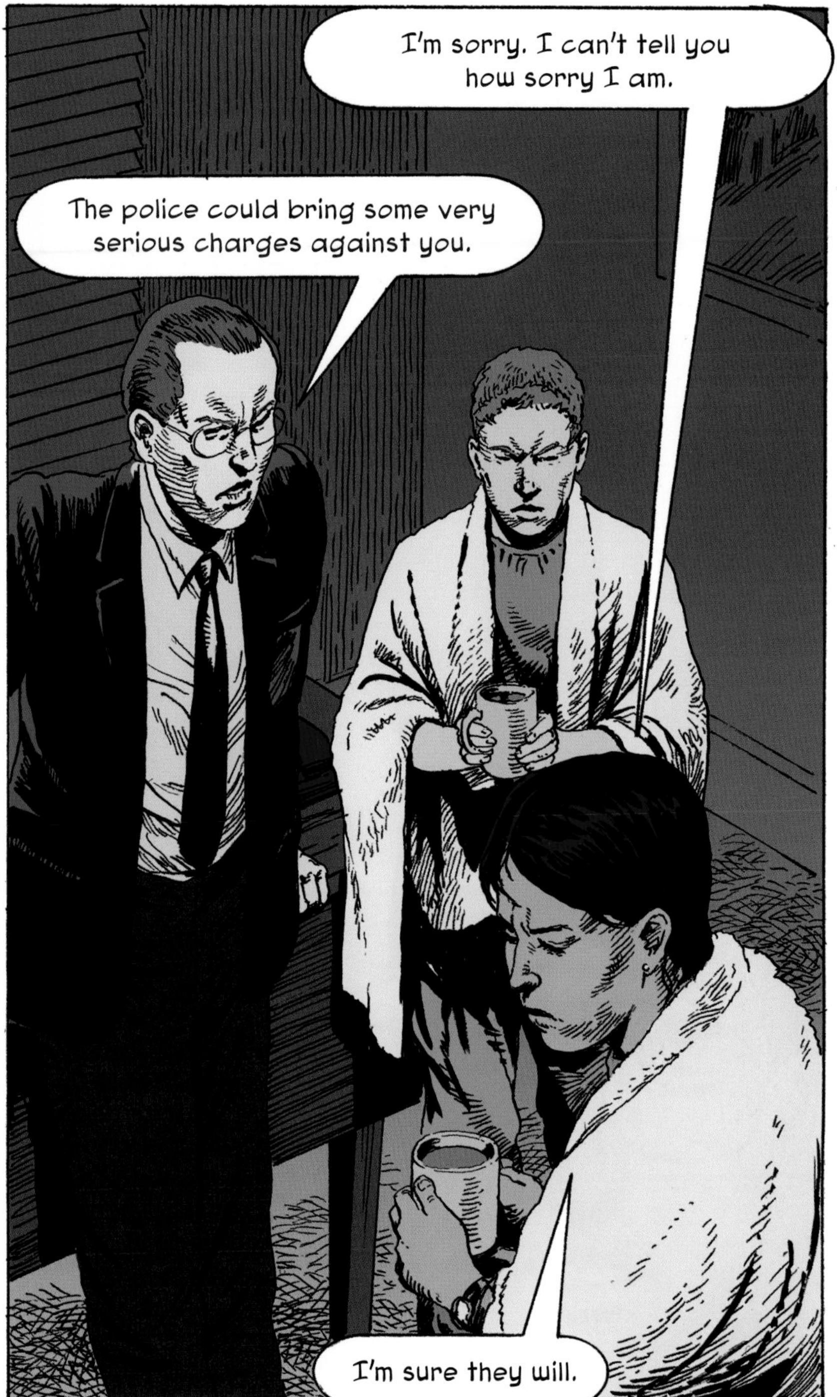
I'm sorry. I can't tell you how sorry I am.
The police could bring some very serious charges against you.
I'm sure they will.

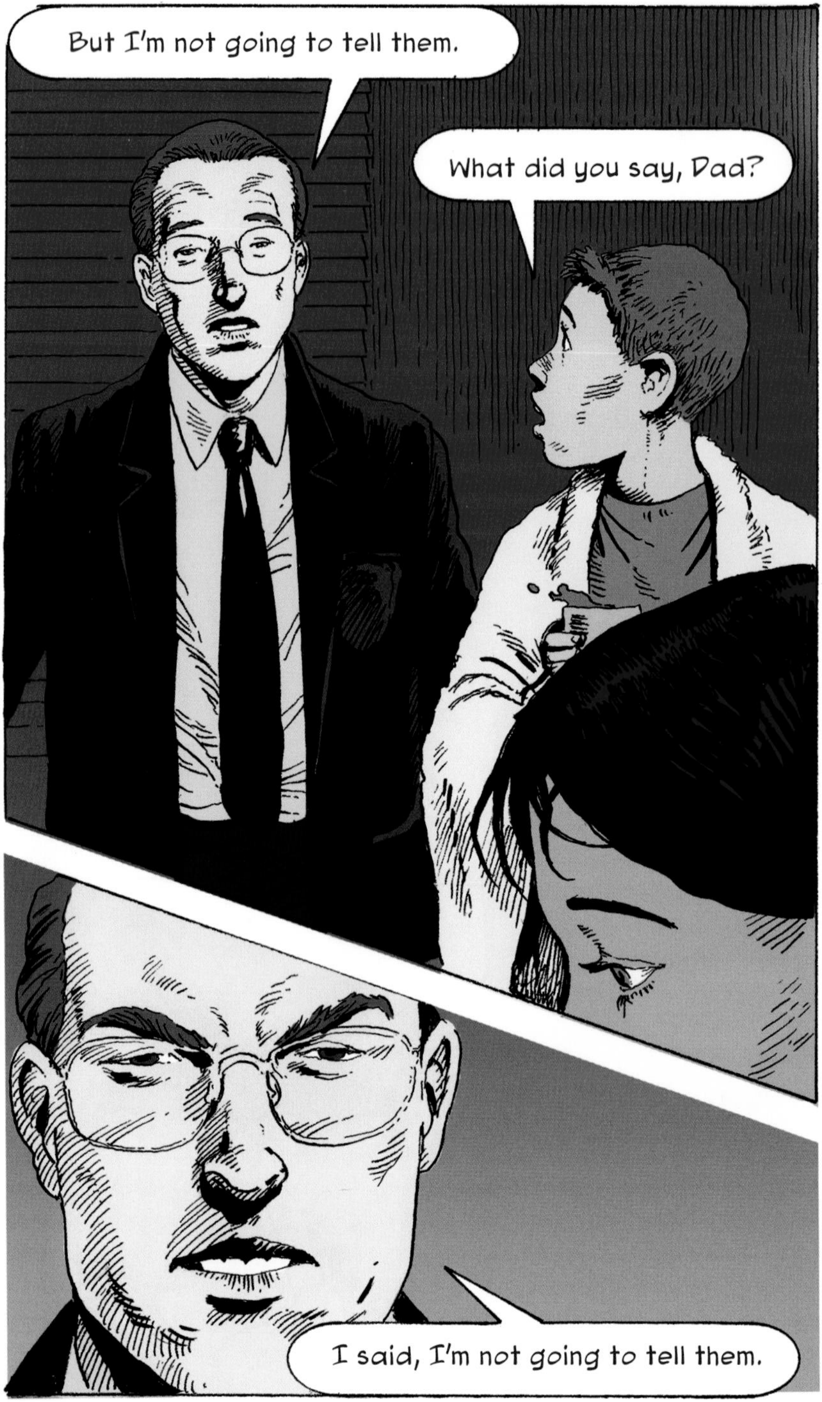
But I'm not going to tell them.
What did you say, Dad?
I said, I'm not going to tell them.

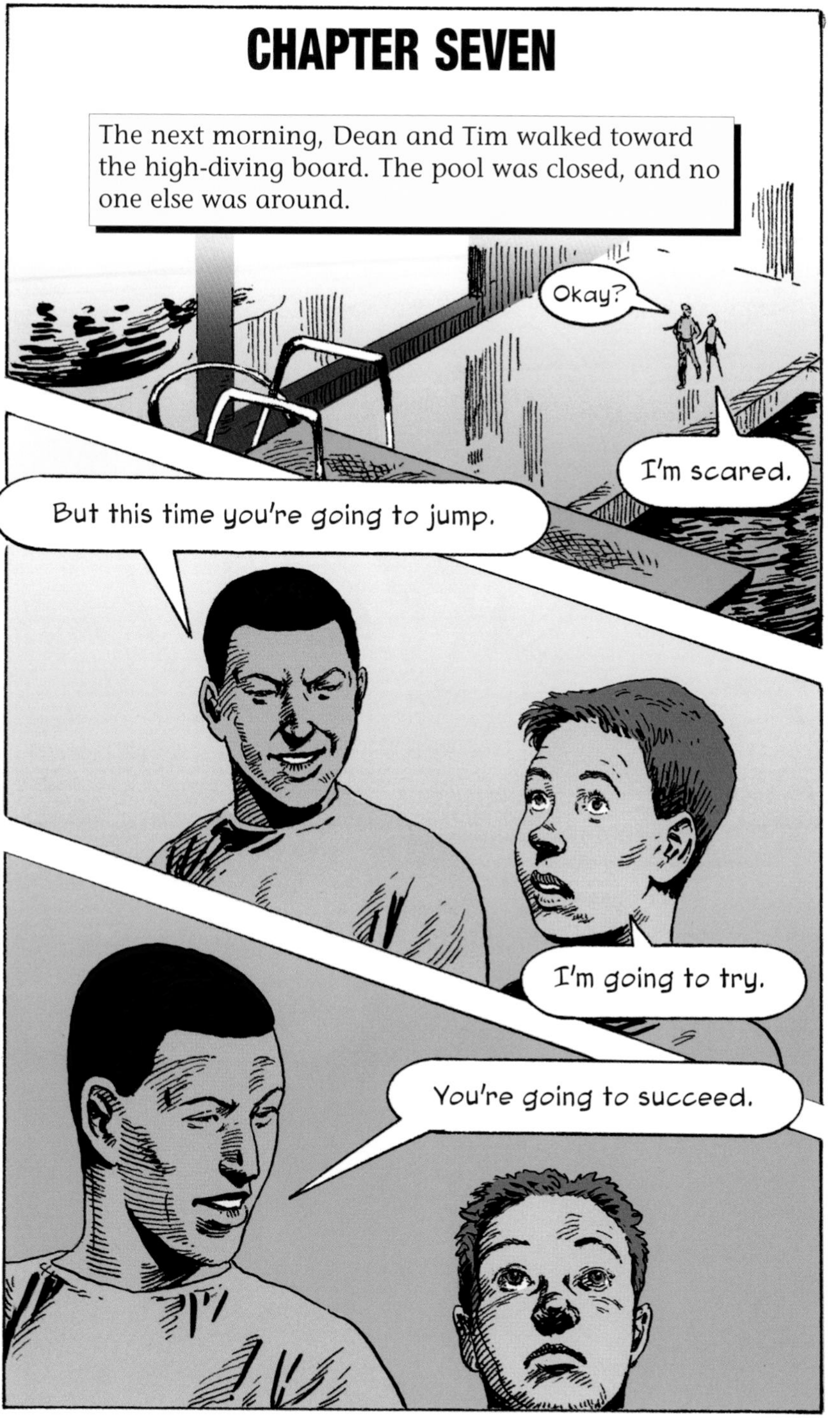
CHAPTER SEVEN
The next morning, Dean and Tim walked toward the high-diving board. The pool was closed, and no one else was around.
Okay?
I'm scared.
But this time you're going to jump.
I'm going to try.
You're going to succeed.

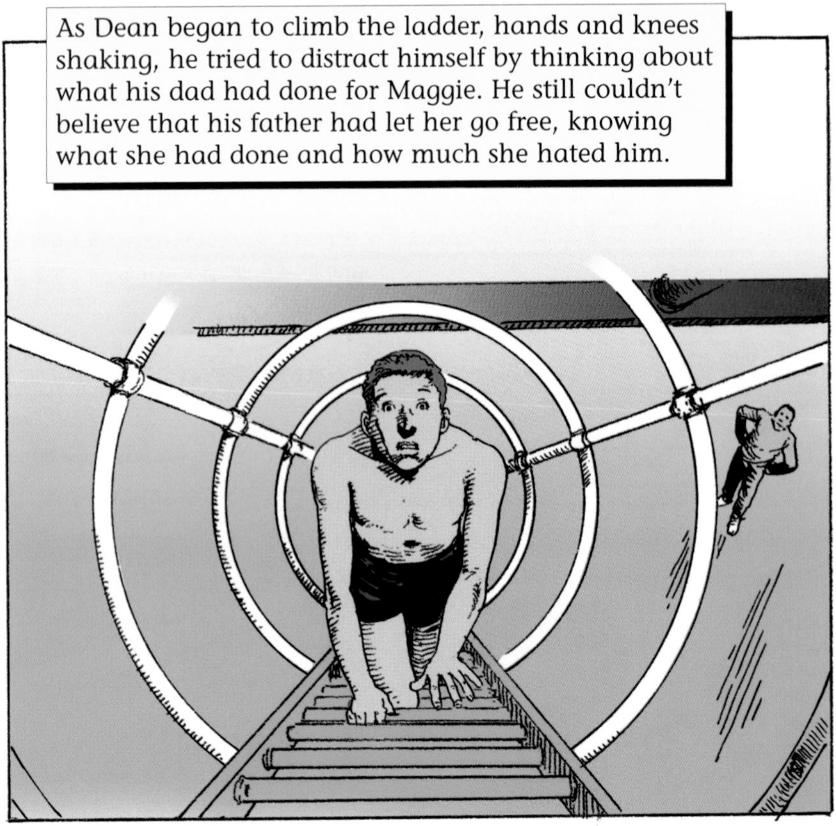
As Dean began to climb the ladder, hands and knees shaking, he tried to distract himself by thinking about what his dad had done for Maggie. He still couldn't believe that his father had let her go free, knowing what she had done and how much she hated him.

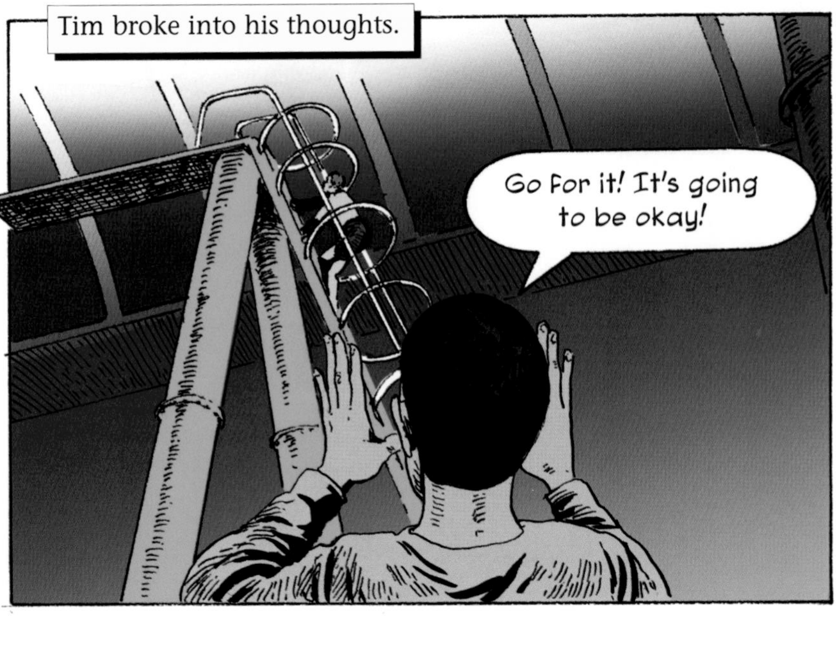
Tim broke into his thoughts.
Go for it! It's going to be okay!

As Dean climbed up, his breath coming in little gasps and sweat pouring down his face, his father's words still rang in his ears.

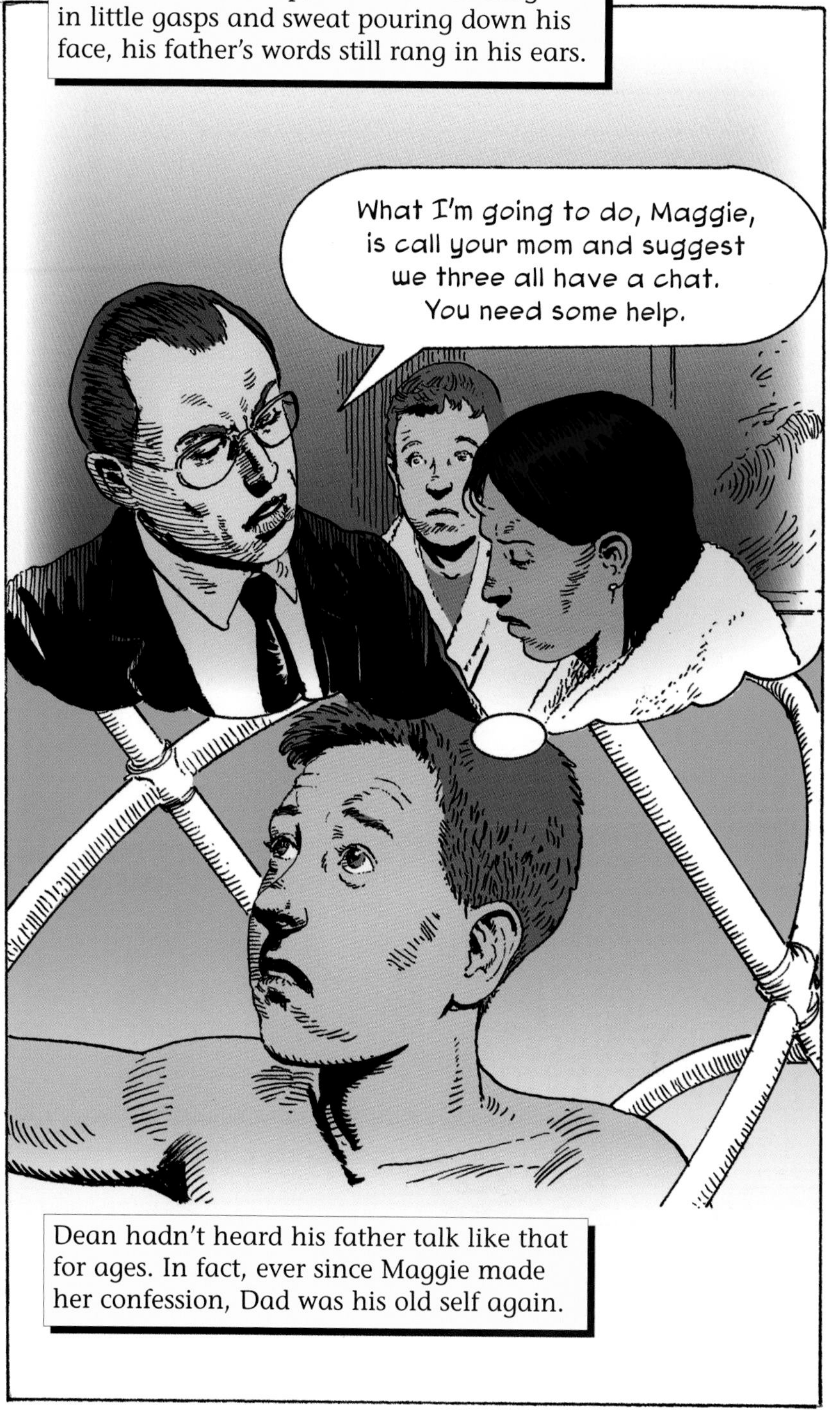
What I'm going to do, Maggie, is call your mom and suggest we three all have a chat. You need some help.

Dean hadn't heard his father talk like that for ages. In fact, ever since Maggie made her confession, Dad was his old self again.

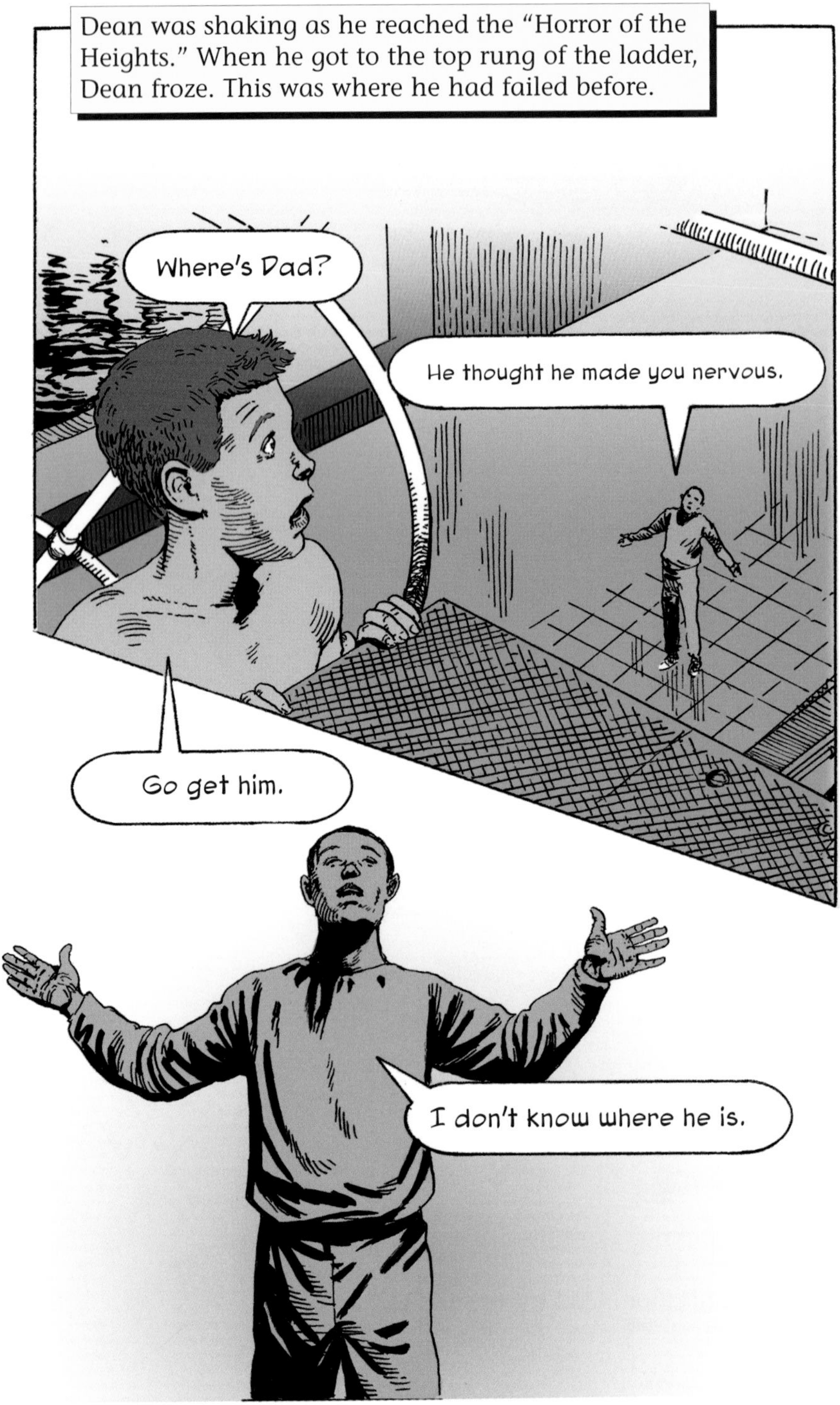
Dean was shaking as he reached the "Horror of the Heights." When he got to the top rung of the ladder, Dean froze. This was where he had failed before.
Where's Dad?
He thought he made you nervous.
Go get him.
I don't know where he is.

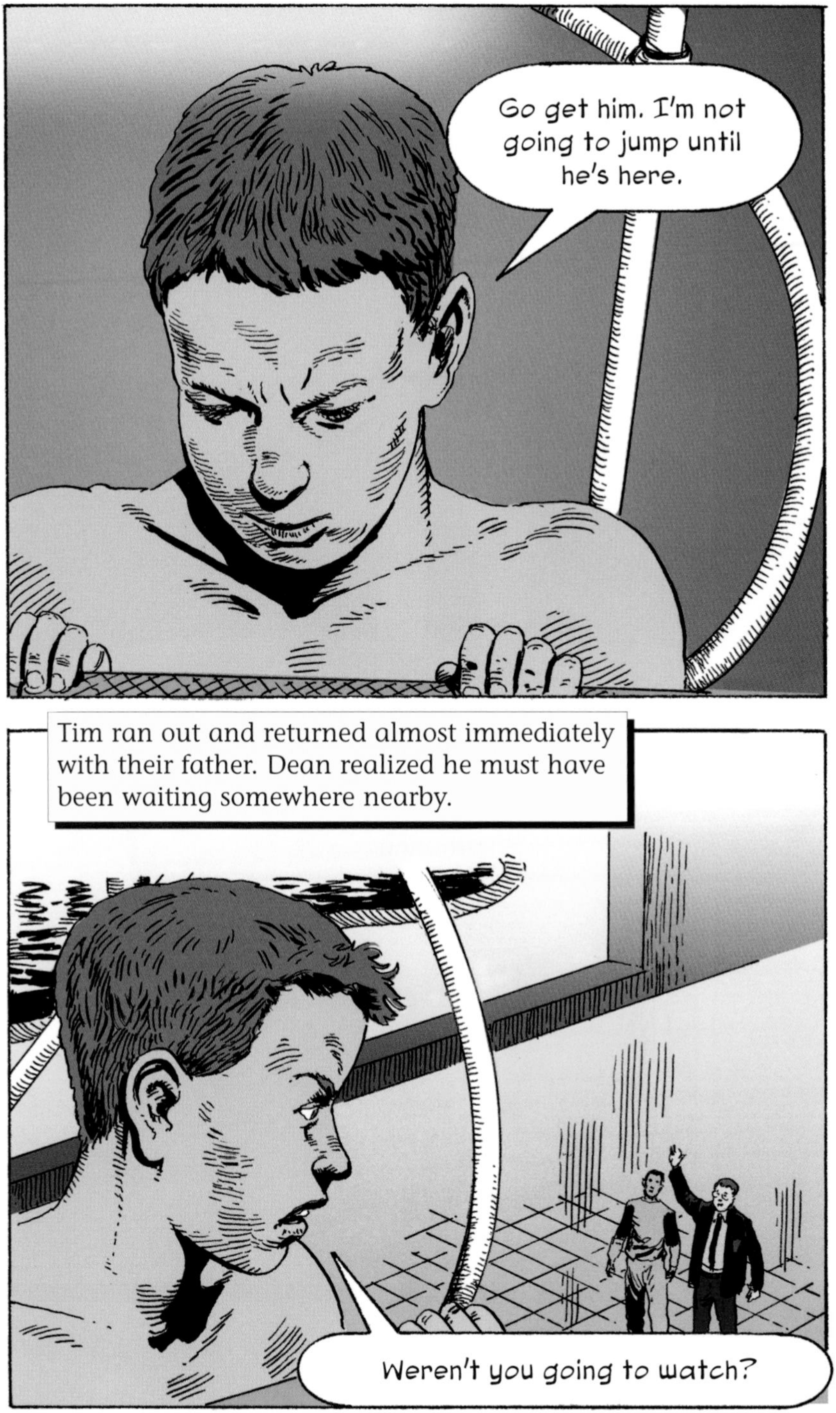
Go get him. I'm not going to jump until he's here.
Tim ran out and returned almost immediately with their father. Dean realized he must have been waiting somewhere nearby.
Weren't you going to watch?

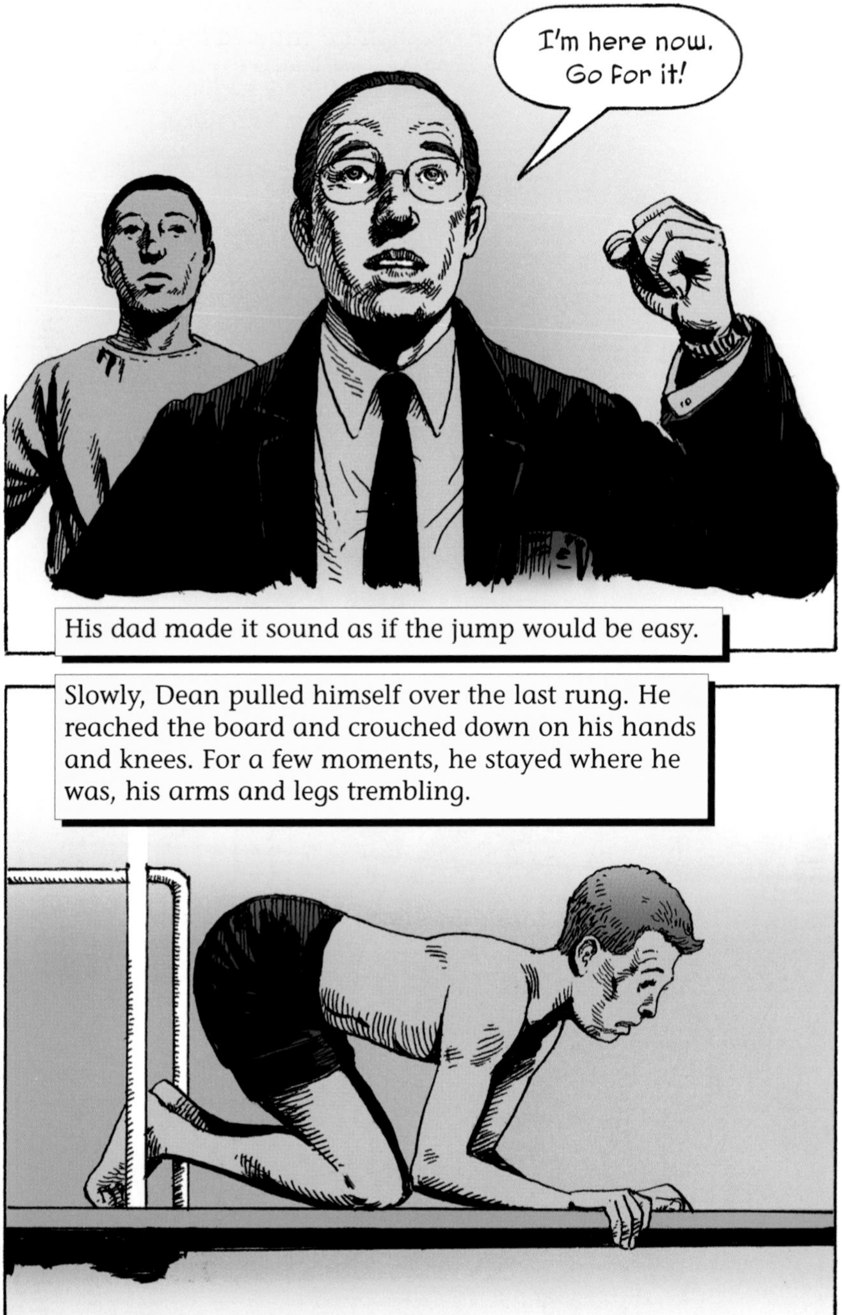
I'm here now. Go for it!
His dad made it sound as if the jump would be easy.
Slowly, Dean pulled himself over the last rung. He reached the board and crouched down on his hands and knees. For a few moments, he stayed where he was, his arms and legs trembling.

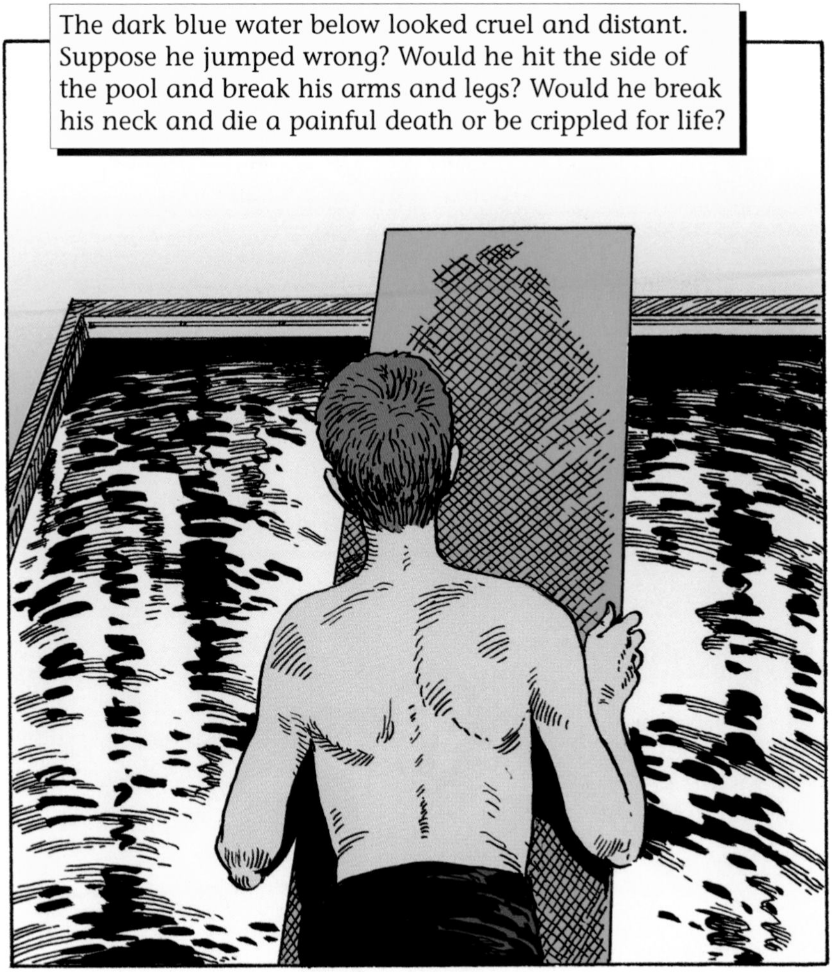
The dark blue water below looked cruel and distant. Suppose he jumped wrong? Would he hit the side of the pool and break his arms and legs? Would he break his neck and die a painful death or be crippled for life?

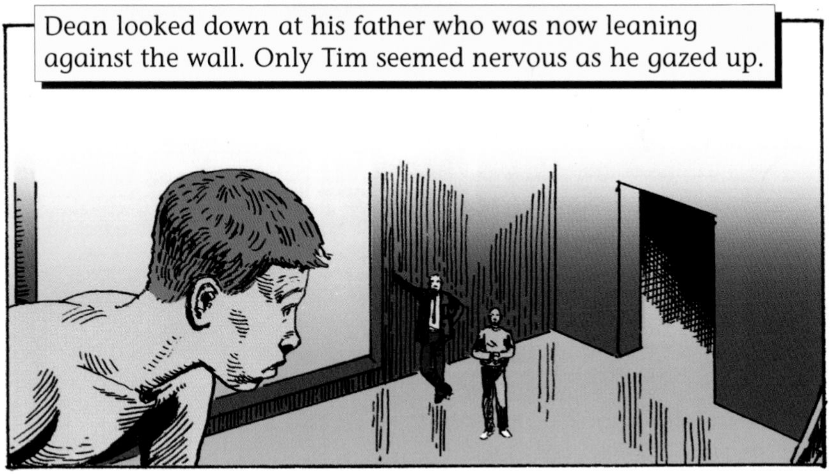
Dean looked down at his father who was now leaning against the wall. Only Tim seemed nervous as he gazed up.

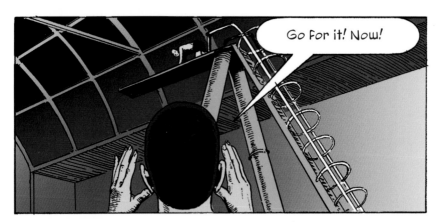

Dean tried to get to his feet, but his arms and legs felt like jelly. He stayed crouching, smelling the chlorine, and listening to the water sloshing against the sides of the pool.

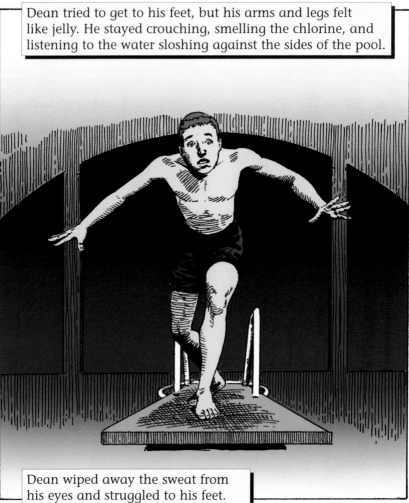

Dean wiped away the sweat from his eyes and struggled to his feet.

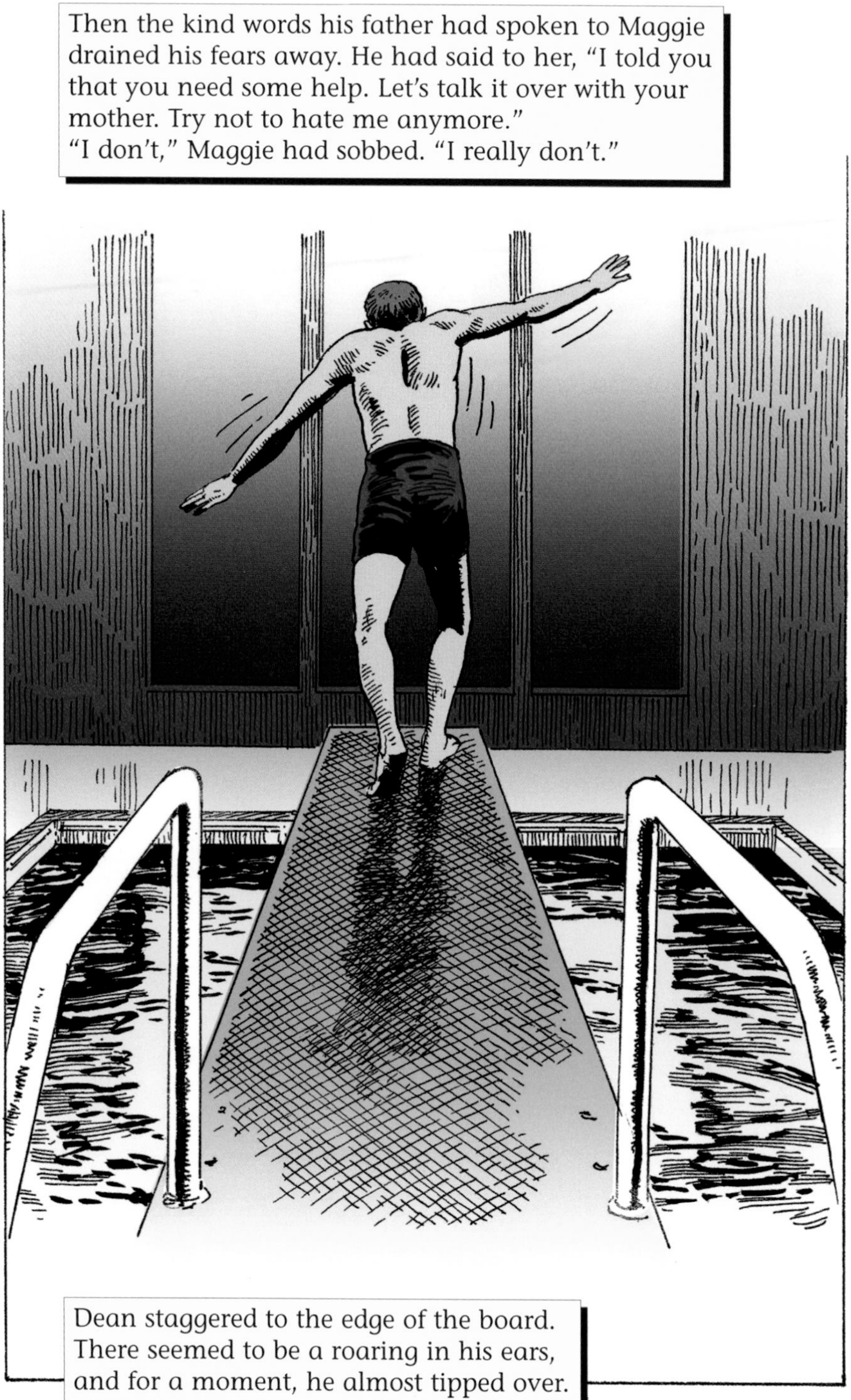
Then the kind words his father had spoken to Maggie drained his fears away. He had said to her, "I told you that you need some help. Let's talk it over with your mother. Try not to hate me anymore."
"I don't," Maggie had sobbed. "I really don't."
Dean staggered to the edge of the board. There seemed to be a roaring in his ears, and for a moment, he almost tipped over.

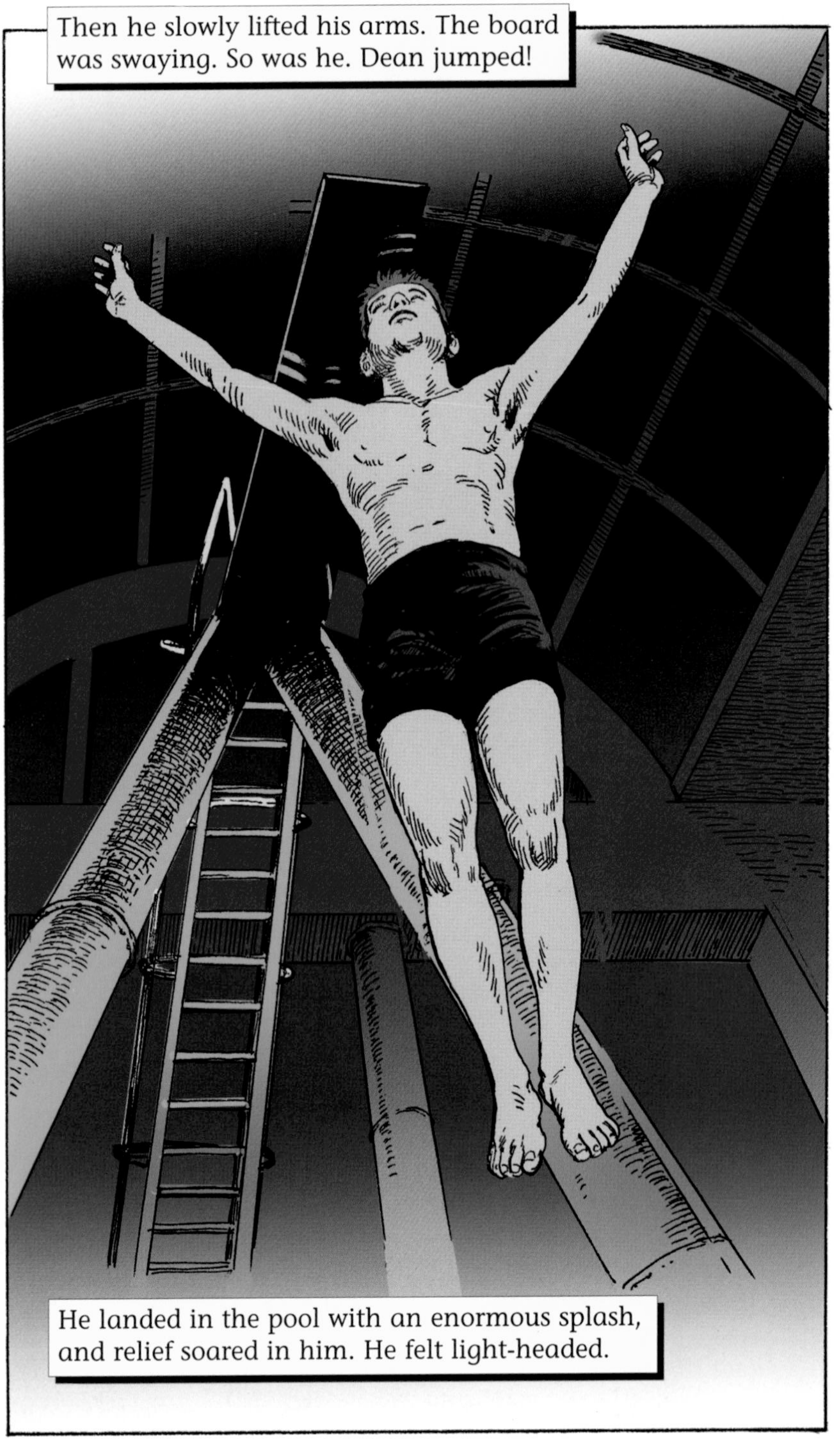
Then he slowly lifted his arms. The board was swaying. So was he. Dean jumped!
He landed in the pool with an enormous splash, and relief soared in him. He felt light-headed.

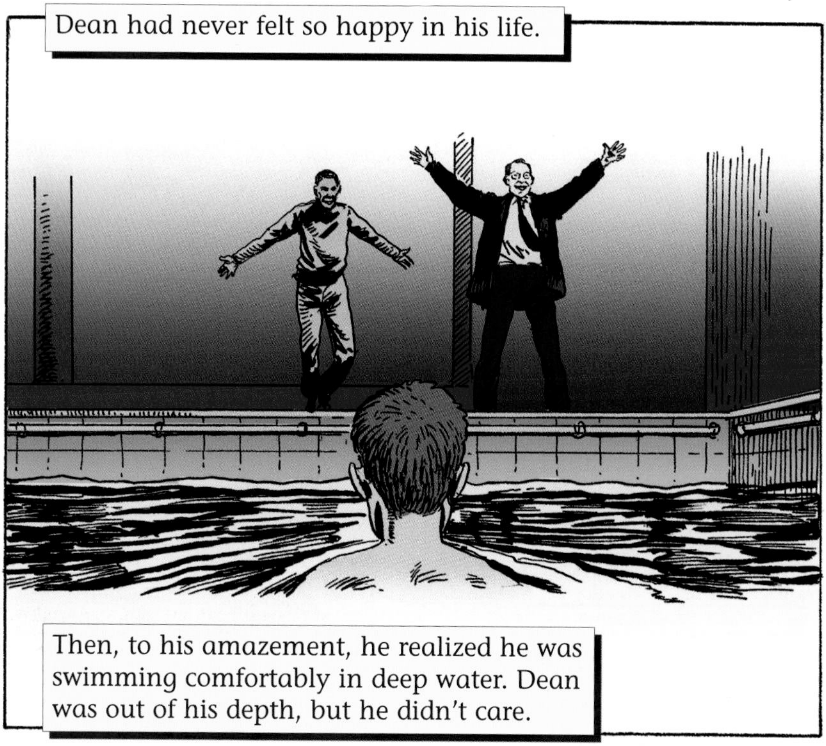
Dean had never felt so happy in his life.
Then, to his amazement, he realized he was swimming comfortably in deep water. Dean was out of his depth, but he didn't care.

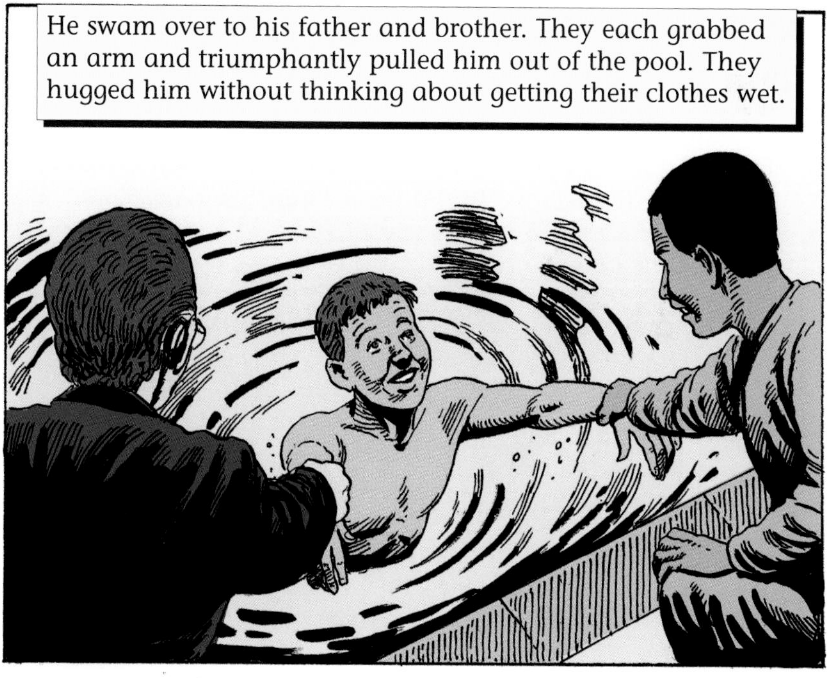
He swam over to his father and brother. They each grabbed an arm and triumphantly pulled him out of the pool. They hugged him without thinking about getting their clothes wet.

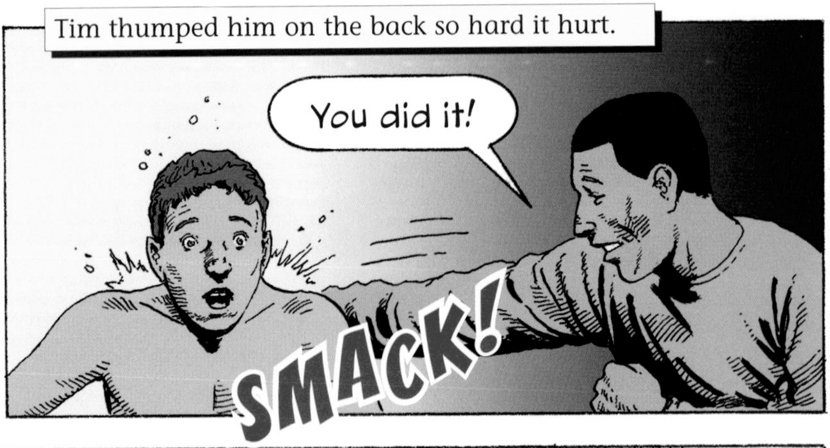
Tim thumped him on the back so hard it hurt.
You did it!
SMACK!

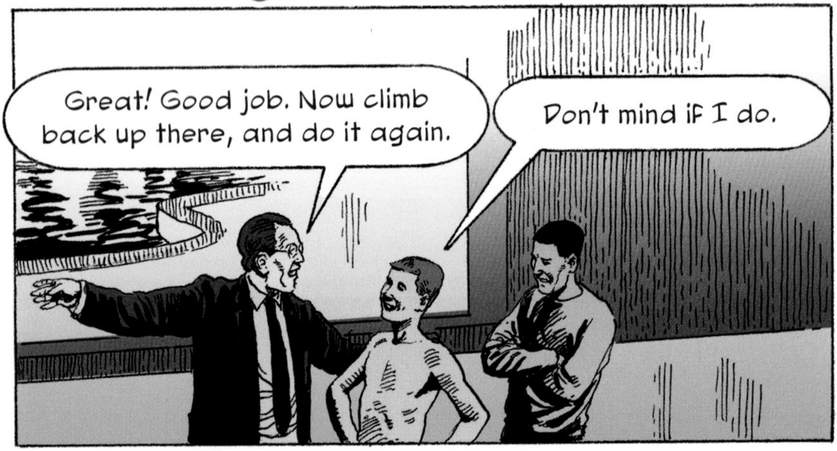
Great! Good job. Now climb back up there, and do it again.
Don't mind if I do.

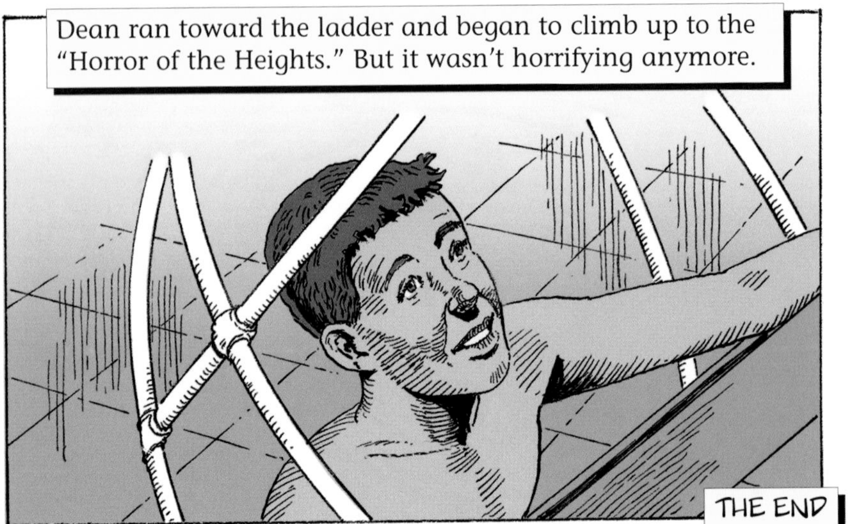
Dean ran toward the ladder and began to climb up to the "Horror of the Heights." But it wasn't horrifying anymore.
THE END

ABOUT THE AUTHOR

Anthony Masters published his first book at age 24. For the rest of his life, he wrote fiction and nonfiction books for children, young adults, and adults. Anthony Masters died in 2003.

GLOSSARY

conquer (KONG-kur)—to defeat something, such as a fear of heights

criticize (KRIT-ih-size)—to find fault

grim (GRIM)—stern or serious

sabotage (SAB-uh-tahzh)—to damage something on purpose

saboteur (sab-uh-TUR)—a person who destroys things

suspicious (suh-SPISH-uhss)—to think something is wrong

INTERNET SITES

Do you want to know more about subjects related to this book? Or are you interested in learning about other topics? Then check out FactHound, a fun, easy way to find Internet sites.

Our investigative staff has already sniffed out great sites for you!

Here's how to use FactHound:

1. Visit *www.facthound.com*

2. Select your grade level.

3. To learn more about subjects related to this book, type in the book's ISBN number: **1598890301**.

4. Click the **Fetch It** button.

FactHound will fetch the best Internet sites for you.

DISCUSSION QUESTIONS

1. Dean thinks that his father hasn't been the same since the car crash. He yells at his sons several times in the book. Why do you think Mr. Lambert is so hard on his sons after the accident?

2. No one suspects Maggie of tampering with the diving board. She suggests that several other people could have done it. Why do you think she suggested these people?

3. Mr. Lambert doesn't call the police on Maggie, even though his son could have been hurt. Why do you think he let her go?

WRITING PROMPTS

1. Dean faced his fears by jumping off the high-diving board. Write about a time when you faced your fears and did something you were scared to do.

2. Revenge is when you try to get back at someone for hurting you. Maggie tried to get revenge on Mr. Lambert by sabotaging his business and hurting his son. Write about a time you tried to get revenge on someone because that person hurt you. Was getting revenge worth it, or did it make you feel worse?

3. Imagine that you are Dean, and Maggie has said she was very sorry and asked for your forgiveness. Write about whether you would forgive her. Why or why not? Could you ever be friends with her again?

ALSO PUBLISHED BY STONE ARCH BOOKS

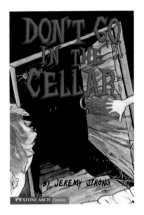

DON'T GO
IN THE
CELLAR
BY JEREMY STRONG
STONE ARCH Fantasy

Don't Go in the Cellar
by Jeremy Strong
1-59889-002-6

Zack finds a warning in his bedroom that tells him not to go down to the cellar. When Laura comes to visit, they go exploring — with disastrous results!

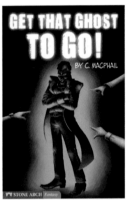

GET THAT GHOST
TO GO!
BY C. MACPHAIL
STONE ARCH Fantasy

Get That Ghost to Go!
by C. MacPhail
1-59889-004-2

Duncan's life is turned upside down when Dean's ghost begins to follow him everywhere.

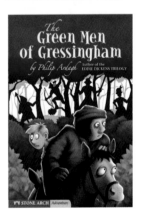

The
Green Men
of Gressingham
by Philip Ardagh
Author of the
EDDIE DICKENS TRILOGY
STONE ARCH Adventure

The Green Men of Gressingham
by Philip Ardagh
1-59889-000-X

The Green Men of Gressingham are medieval outlaws. When a new tax is introduced, they turn to kidnapping!

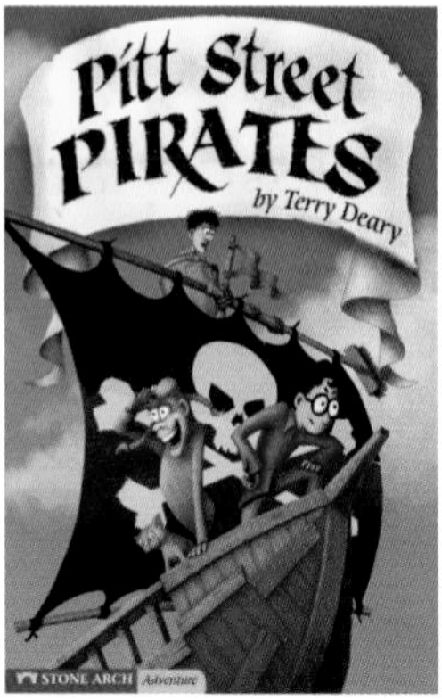
Pitt Street
PIRATES
by Terry Deary
STONE ARCH

Pitt Street Pirates
by Terry Deary
1-59889-005-0

Will these modern-day pirates be able to outwit the spoiled rich kids?

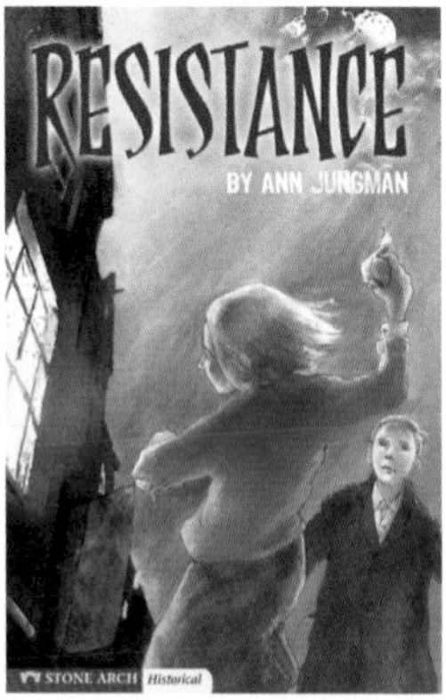
RESISTANCE
BY ANN JUNGMAN
STONE ARCH

Resistance
by Ann Jungman
1-59889-001-8

Jan is ashamed when his father sides with the Germans during World War II. Can he and his best friend secretly help the Resistance?

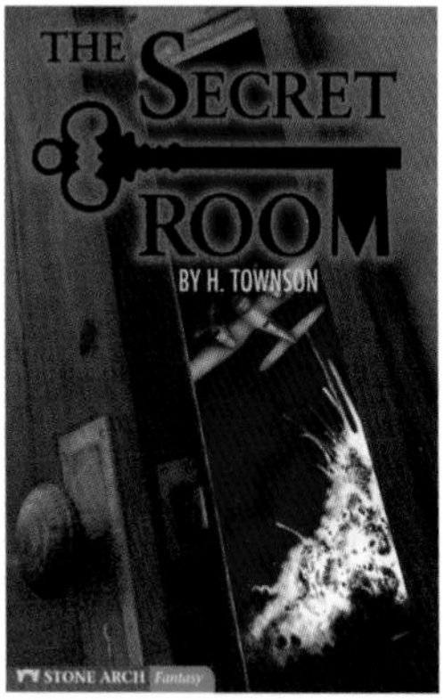
THE
SECRET
ROOM
BY H. TOWNSON
STONE ARCH

The Secret Room
by H. Townson
1-59889-003-4

Adam suddenly finds himself in a very different world, one in which he could be in terrible danger.

ALSO BY ANTHONY MASTERS

JOKER
by Anthony Masters
WHO KIDNAPPED MAGIC MAX?
STONE ARCH Graphic Novel

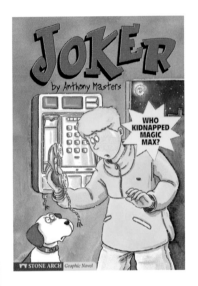

Joker
1-59889-024-7

When Mel's dad, Magic Max, is kidnapped, no one believes him. Everyone thinks it's just another one of his jokes. Can Mel find the kidnappers by himself?

ORDER NOW!

STONE ARCH BOOKS,
151 Good Counsel Hill Drive, Mankato, MN 56001
1-800-421-7731
www.stonearchbooks.com